DEAR MATT —

YOUR DADDY IS

GREAT!

Love
MASTERD

Hey God—
Are You Really Really Up There?

Hey God—
Are You Really Really Up There?

A Novel by

Malcolm Perkins

DORRANCE PUBLISHING CO., INC.
PITTSBURGH, PENNSYLVANIA 15222

ISBN # 0-8059-6089-9
Printed in the United States of America

First Printing

For information or to order additional books, please write:
Dorrance Publishing Co., Inc.
701 Smithfield Street
Third Floor
Pittsburgh, Pennsylvania 15222-3906
U.S.A.
1-800-788-7654
Or visit our web site and on-line catalog at www.dorrancepublishing.com

To some penguin in the arctic, and some hyena maybe in Africa. I'm sure God knows that they both exist. But I'm just not so sure that the penguin or the hyena know or care that I exist. Anyway, to my Ryan, *that's* for absolutely certain.

Prologue

I am writing *now*, what happened to me some twenty or so years ago. I am older now, and, I hope, a bit wiser. I have more wrinkles now, and my teeth are surely looser, but I have the answers to questions now that I didn't have back then. So being *fifty-four* isn't all *that* bad. My name is Walter Edward Stillman. My friends and family simply call me Walt. I hope I don't have any enemies, but if I do, or did, they'd probably call me Wally. This is my story and how, in my mid-thirties, in a short, *six month* period of my life, everything that possibly could go wrong—did—and then some! Probably Murphy's Law times a zillion. And Murphy *wasn't* a parrot.

I *cannot* tell you the whys or the hows of that six-month period some twenty years ago—Ys are crooked letters anyway. It just friggin' happened. It could have happened to any of us, but for whatever reason or reasons, it happened *to me*. My whole life suddenly, out of nowhere, was stomped on, trampled on, and loudly and grotesquely turned inside and out. There were *no* warnings—*no* days or nights. I had *no* feeling in my limbs, and my heart was cold like granite. I couldn't eat and there was to be no sleep. I wouldn't wish what happened to me back then on any living soul or any non-living soul.

My beautiful wife, whom I had loved since high school, was suddenly killed. *Before* my wife, by about fifty-eight days or so, my young son also senselessly died. My daughter, just a wee bit older than my son, began to stutter terribly. Nerves—the doctors back then, told me it was her nerves. I had lost a job that I had labored at and treasured and had had since high school. I began to drink—a lot, then more than a lot. And one night, while working a part-time job to get money for bills, I hit an elderly couple with my car. A couple who had never hurt a soul. Of course, my car insurance had lapsed by about a week. And I began to get these awful attacks where my heart would pound and my eyes would bulge. Nerves—again, they used that term. They told me that there was nothing physically wrong, I was simply having a *panic* attack. I remember back then, that I *almost* gave up. Maybe I was supposed to suffer. Maybe I was supposed to tell my story. Maybe I was supposed to get the answers that I finally got. Maybe a lot of things.

Chapter I

In the Beginning

Anyway, this is my story, exactly as it all happened to me some twenty years ago now. Like I just told you, my name is Walter Edward Stillman. Most of those who know and care for me call me Walt—plain ol' Walt. *Not* Wally and *not* junior. My dad, of course, had the identical name. I'm fifty-four now, and my horror happened about twenty years ago at about age thirty-four. But to tell it to you right, I'd have to go *way* back—to my birth. To the very things that made me the *what* and the *who* of what I am all about.

September 25, 1942! That was to be my howdy-do to the dust bowl state of Kansas. Western Kansas to be exact. To me, Kansas is a great state. And no matter what, I'll always love it. It's near Oklahoma, Colorado, and Nebraska and sometimes it's almost forgotten, but *not* by me—never! And not just because I was born there. We're pretty famous for beef and agriculture, but to tell you the truth, our *wheat* is this nation's finest. I'm real real proud of that, too. To be number one at *anything* takes a lot of doing.

Anyway, my parents and my parent's parents, and their parents, to some extent, dabbled in wheat. Like any state, Kansas has its share of buildings, cities, graveyards, tunnels, and the like. But *we* Kansians also have this special spirit. I can't really explain it, but we in Kansas darn sure have it. I'm probably just prejudiced, but that's okay too. I don't really know too much about our state's history, or *any* history for that matter. But I do know that our state was a part of the great Louisiana Purchase from France. What a great deal that was! So

1

much was bought for so little. I guess at that very time, the French needed the money. If you ask me, some people will do some pretty awful and crazy things for the sake of the almighty dollar. Not me, and not all people—just some people.

Anyway, like I said, I was born in western Kansas, September 25, 1942. I don't know how many towns or cities are in our state, but I surely know the *one* I grew up in, *Lomar*—Lomar, Kansas. That's where *everything* happened—right there in Lomar—where the meadowlark is the friggin' bird and the sunflower is the friggin' flower. Hey, I told you just before that some people will do some pretty awful things for the sake of money. It's a sad truth, but a truth nonetheless. Down the way a bit from the farm where I grew up, when I was I guess eleven or so, this awful awful, awful thing happened. They said at that time that it was the most horrible crime in our Lomar history. And it was all about what I was just talking about before—some people doing almost *anything* for money.

This nice couple, the Fentons, and their two beautiful kids lived on a farm. It wasn't a big farm, and it wasn't a little farm either. It was right near the swimming hole that we all used to plunge buck naked in when the Kansas sun hit 105 degrees or so. Everything was proper about the Fenton's farm, if you know what I mean. The silo, the rooster on the roof, the stretching fields—the everything. Everybody liked the Fentons. They were givers, believed in the Lord, and they for darn sure, earned an honest day's pay on their simple farm. But, one night, as everyone slept, some creeps—for money, or what they thought was money—just upped and ended it all. They slaughtered the whole entire family. At the time, back then, it made TV and the newspapers everywhere. Not because of the fact that there was a murder in Lomar, Kansas, but because of the *why* and the *how* of such a senseless and brutal act.

The creeps who did it, tied everyone up, parents, kids, and even their dog, then cut all of their throats, doused them with gasoline, and finally set them all on fire. But why? Surely not for the one hundred bucks that was taken. Even now, when I think about it, I get the worse case of goose bumps. I guess you all will have to get used to me doing *that*. You know, talking about one thing, and then, out of nowhere, rambling over to another. I mean, there I was talking about the great

Louisiana Purchase, and about the people doing stupid things for the almighty dollar, and bam—the Fenton story just upped and came out. Hey, that's just the way I am.

Yes, I had grandparents. To tell you the truth, I don't remember them a whole heck of a lot. But I do remember them a little, and I guess remembering a little is better than not remembering at all. My grandparents, all four of them, were true Kansians in every stretch of the word. They were all born in the latter part of the *nineteenth* century, which would have been *after* Paul Revere yet *before* JFK. Values were different back then; naturally so were a lot of other things. People got by even without TVs and without McDonalds. The stars were still bright in the heavens, lilacs still smelled delicious, and Christmas was still a big event.

I remember my *mother's* parents most of all. My grandmom's name was *Jenny*, and my pop-pop's name was *Louis*. Appropriate names for your grandparents, if you ask me. *She* was a seamstress and *he* was a tailor. What I remember most about my mom's parents was that *he* had this huge handlebar mustache and always wore a vest with a watch in the pocket, and *she* had really pretty silver hair always up in a bun, and her glasses were always hanging from around her neck.

I never really did get a chance to know my *dad's* parents, but they must have been real good people, because my dad is a just and honorable man. And it's my opinion, for what it's worth, that the apple usually falls somewhere close to its tree. Not *all* the time, but usually! Anyway, my mom-mom and my pop-pop on my mom's side lived for a long, long time, seamstressing and tailoring and living and loving. The only seamstress that I had ever heard of *before* my mom-mom, was good ol' Betsy Ross. And then I found out that another person, *not* Betsy, probably made our country's first flag.

It was to be my pop-pop on my father's side, who was to be my first grandparent to just up and die. And I guess that *his* death, was to be my real first experience with subjects like *humans* or *God* or *life* or *dying*. I can't really count my childhood dog *Weepy*, because he was human only to me, and though I was devastated by Weepy's death, it still just *wasn't* the same, as a human death. Before my dad's dad died, I believed that the people you truly loved simply lived forever. I figured why would God do anything to ever hurt any living soul? That's *not* what the Bible was supposed to be all about! Yes, I had read the Bible, and I knew about the flood, and I knew about God asking Abraham to kill his only son, Isaac, but, I figured, there just *had* to be a reason—there just *had* to be. Little did I know *back then*, what God, for whatever reason or reasons, had in store *for me later* in *my* life.

Anyway, my pop-pop's funeral on my father's side really scared me when I was a kid. He looked so small and so helpless in that coffin he was jammed in. It all looked so friggin' *final*. His head was tilted back on a white satin pillow and they had placed something religious in his hands. That whole experience gave me the willies and a chill that I'll never ever forget.

Anyway, I don't want you to get confused about something. There was *another* murder in my state of Kansas that was about *another* family, *not* the Fentons. They even wrote a book and made a movie about it. Something about *cold blood*, but for sure, they *weren't* one and the same. To me, my state of Kansas was and still is, the best. The spirit, the heat, the people, the everything. Oh sure, it's a *dust* state too. At times it gets really, really bad, but so what! Kansas is no different than any other state where hurricanes rip you or earthquakes shake you. It's not something you like, but taking the good with the bad, you just have to learn to live with it. There's about five billion or so of us humans on this planet, and I'm sure that there is no place that is *absolutely* perfect.

Sometimes out of nowhere, even at fifty-four, I ask myself strange questions. Like, what's the world's worst job? Or what would it be like to be the planet's last survivor? To tell you the truth, sometimes I even talk to myself. Just to sort of get things straight, but I'm sure that by me doing that, there's no harm done. And after all I've been through, and I guess after all is said and done, I'm allowed! Besides, the Ys of our world are crooked letters anyway.

After my grandparents, Louis and Jenny, on my mom's side, and the two on my dad's, came of course, *my* parents. Unlike my grandparents, my parents were born in the *twentieth* century, but they, too, were *Kansas* bred and born. And to this day, they are both still alive and kicking. My dad's name is Walter *Sr.*— that's why I never really liked Wally or Junior. And my mom's name is Melinda. Two of the finest people who ever walked the planet Earth. They aren't big shots or uppity or above anybody. Two good people, that's just who they are. My mom used to love to cook, and boy, could she! And my dad, Walter Sr., loved to work our farm, fiddle with woodcraft, and smoke his pipe. I can still to this day, taste my mom's cooking and smell my dad's fine pipe. There are some things that you just never, ever forget. Or ever want to.

Our farm was called *"the Stillman Farm,"* as that was, of course, our last name. And what a farm it was. *Old MacDonald* had nothing over us. We had cows, pigs, ducks, horses, and all kinds of crops. And *wheat!* Lots and lots of wheat. I was the only child, and I did all of the farm chores I was supposed to. And I loved every minute of doing them. I felt that I belonged, and nothing was too much or too dirty for me to do. I swept, I cleaned, I tended to our animals, I painted— I did it all. And what I didn't know how to do, my dad Walter, with love, taught me. I loved him back *then*, and I love him *now*—a lot! He's probably, and always has been, my best friend. He's always been there for me, through thick and thin. He never judged me or yelled. He always backed me up ten million percent. And for sure, as you'll learn later, there certainly were the *thin* times!

Like I told you, I was born into this world September 25, 1942, a *Friday*. I have often wondered why there are only *seven* days in a week and not eight or maybe even nine. And if there were, you know, an eighth, what would they call it? I told you, *I* think about *stuff* like that. Anyway, on that particular day, September 25, 1942, many historical things happened. And though, for sure, I'm *not* a history buff, I did make it a point, somewhere in my teens, to research what actually did happen around our great nation upon *my* exact entrance into civilization. One of the great newspapers in New York begged for the United States to *awaken* because we were losing the war. Somewhere in the state of Maryland, on the east coast, twenty people died in a bad fire of three B&O trains. And in baseball, the great Mel Ott was the Phillies manager. I guess history— though I'm not a great follower, except for my birth—can teach us so much. In fact if anyone ever asked me to choose *any time* at all to go back to, *any time* at all, I'd have to ask to go back to the very *first* day. I mean, the *real* very first day! What really and truly happened on that very first day? Were there really an Adam and Eve? Or a garden of anything? Or was there first this gigantic bang, and then everything just happened? I told you before, that *I* simply like to think about stuff like that, like what if *this* or what if *that*. Like if I could pick one person who ever lived to be like, who would I choose? It'd probably be Davy Crockett—and I don't know why, but it just would!

So on September 25, 1942, I was born right there, on our Stillman Farm. Amidst all the history going on, probably ducks quacking, amidst *everything*. From what my parents told me, and from what early pictures show, I was a particularly happy baby. It's hard for me now, at fifty-four, to remember all of my early early years. But I surely remember our farm, my grandparents, my parents, our farm animals, some of my early friends, and of course, my mom's great cooking and my dad's great-smelling pipe. And I also remember *Weepy*, my faithful childhood dog, who, like I already told you, has of course long ago since died. I'd have to say except for *those* things, the first *five* or so years of my life, to me now, are almost blank. I'm sure if I really had to, or if I somehow got hypnotized, I would surely remember a bit more, but until then, sorry as I am, I can only remember really from my *fifth* year or so of my life as I now know it.

I do remember in detail my *sixth* birthday party at our family farm. I also remember my very very, first kid school, and of course, my very, very first girlfriend. Her name was Gretchen Mullen, and she was seven and I was six. I also loved to play that old kid game, kickball. I liked *that* a lot. I might be rambling, but to tell you my life story as it really happened, rambling, for me, just might be a necessity. I also remember from those younger years my uncle Karl, my father's youngest brother. He smoked cigars, big stinky ones, all the time. He used to lift me up in the air a lot, that seemed to be his thing, and when he did, I could always smell those horrible cigars. But I had no hard feelings toward him, *then* or *now*. In fact, when I went through what I went through, you know, in my thirties, my uncle Karl was behind me and by my side every step of the way.

Anyway, my first years of life as a west Kansian weren't really out of the ordinary. I did whatever a kid would do or wouldn't do who lived on a farm. I wasn't tall and I wasn't small, I wasn't loud and I wasn't shy. I guess I just *was*!

Chapter II

Those Young Years

I loved my dog Weepy. I loved my parents, and I loved our Stillman Farm. And I guess, by a teeny kid's standard, I must have loved my first girlfriend, Gretchen, too! I do remember in detail, *vivid* detail, one incident that happened to me in those, my young years. We were all at our favorite swimming hole near the Fenton farm, that farm where horror had recently struck. All of us guys were behind the bushes, and all of the girls were getting ready to skinny dip. I peeked out to catch a look-see at all of their naked white tushies. I knew that I shouldn't have, and then suddenly *it* happened! I felt this quick sting in my right foot, and of course I was barefoot. When I looked down to see what had stung me, I saw this squiggly, horrible *snake*, and I knew immediately that I had been snake zapped. This was to be the first and only snake zap of my entire life. Funny, though, when you are young like I was, you don't really get that crazy or that scared when horrible things just up and happen to you. Maybe that's because you are just *that* young or because, in the back of your young mind, you are convinced that somehow or someway your parents will absolutely always make things A-okay. Hey, of course I recovered— I'm here—but that was one experience of my west Kansian youth that I'll never, ever forget.

They say, or *some* say, that we have many lives that come before our present one. So I'm sure, like I said before, that if I ever got hyp-notized or something, maybe I could find out more, like perhaps that I was the most famous kickball player in ancient Greece. But to tell

7

you the gospel, I really *don't* want to do that. I can remember back far enough to please me, like to things like my cigar-smoking Uncle Karl or my very famous snakebite. To go back really really further, perhaps to a past life, if there really was one, would be to mess with stuff that I really don't want to mess with.

Anyway, I was about twelve or so in my beloved Lomar, Kansas, when I experienced, face to face, my very first *twister.* And, now, looking back all those years, I do have to truly say that it was ugly, scary, awesome, beautiful, and terrifying, all at the same time. I told you before, I'm sure, that in Lomar, we were right smack-dab in the middle of the famous dust bowl. But, unhappily, *twisters* lived there, too. However nature's stuff really happens everywhere, surely not just in Kansas. Maybe us people who live in places where nature sometimes rules like to live on the edge. Or maybe, like that TV commercial once said, we like the thrill of victory and the agony of defeat. Or maybe we all had no friggin' choice. It's just simply the way our *watchmakers*—you know, our parents and their parents—simply made it all happen.

Anyway, about that terrifying yet beautiful twister. My family was *somewhat* prepared. We had built a shelter and had it for years and years. In fact, we simply called it "the twister shelter." It was nothing really fancy, but a shelter nonetheless. Hey, *that day* it all just happened so, so fast. We were eating dinner, and we all sensed something was coming. The TV had announced the probability and we had our shelter, so there wasn't much more that we could do. The whole twister lasted only a minute or so. We never made it outside to the shelter. And it probably was the longest minute of all of our lives. We almost, in that minute, lost *everything.* I know that sounds impossible but, we almost did. Even the wooden rooster on top of our barn door.

That was to be the first time that I saw my dad Walter Sr., cry. And *that* really bothered me. I can still remember it now. There was all of our tower of strength, my dad, crawling on all fours on the floor, picking things up and trying in vain to stick them back together. And he was sobbing as he did it. Back then, I remember, we all clung on to each other. I had read about the Great Depression—and about that horrible stock market crash. But that twister was right *there*, right *then*, and it was happening to *us.*

Anyway, my family stuck together, and we got through it—love can do so much. That ol' twister just wasn't going to beat us—it just wasn't! Looking back now, I guess those, my young years, with my uncle Karl, my snakebite, of course Gretchen, kickball, and even that twister, taught me stuff, even though I didn't realize it at the time, that surely in one way or another would help me later in life.

Chapter III

High School

Junior high, at about age thirteen, was simply junior high. Nothing really *that* special, nothing really *that* bad. I learned a little bit of this and a little bit of that. It was in *high school* where my life was to get its beginning.

I went to *Lomar High School*, not too far from our farm, and really not too far from anything. It really looked just like a high school was supposed to look. It even *smelled* like a high school, if you know what I mean. It had a huge steeple with a clock, and you could see it from miles away. And of course there were hallways, a cafeteria, a gym, and teachers. Lomar High had lots and lots of teachers.

Being a freshman wasn't really that bad. If you think about it, we are *always* a freshman in one way or another—a freshman in life, and then finally a freshman when we up and die. I guess that's just a given. My high school was almost like any other high school—I say *almost*, because to me, then and even now, it was the best of the best. My grades weren't the greatest, but I did my very best, and that's all my parents asked of me, and all I really asked of myself. I gave all of my courses my best shot, and I never ever missed a single day of school— not *one* out of all four years. They gave me some sort of award for it when I graduated. Look, there was no doubt about it—I'd probably never ever get the Nobel or the Pulitzer, but for sure I used to dream anyway. Like about finding the cure for cancer, or maybe even becoming vice president of our great county. Funny, now that I look back at it all, I never dreamed about becoming *president*, only *vice* president.

At Lomar High, there were the usual clubs and fraternities, but they never really interested me. I sort of flew solo, and I liked it that way.

Then in my freshman year, *it* just upped and happened. Out of nowhere, I, Walt Stillman, was to be changed forever.

Outside of the principal's office, where all the students could see it, there hung this *huge sign*. It was on a white background with big bold black letters. And read: BASEBALL TRYOUTS TODAY— REPORT TO COACH RAY! *Seven* words, that's all there were. Seven words that were to change my life forever.

To tell you the gospel, I had never, up to that point in my life, the point where I had seen that sign, ever really given a single thought to baseball. Or any ball for that matter. Oh sure, I had played kickball, and I had tossed different kinds of balls and objects through an old tire that my dad had hung from a chain on our farm. But *that* was the extent up to that point of my baseball life. I did a lot of other *boy* stuff, and I loved to work woodcraft with my dad. And as far as that old hanging tire, I was never much good at getting *anything* smack dab through the middle. Of course I had heard all about Babe Ruth and the Mick. Who hadn't?

Anyway, as my story goes, I remember that very *first* practice like it was only yesterday. I wasn't really nervous, because I didn't think I had the slightest chance to make the team. I didn't know why I even went. I guess, looking back now, it was just to be one of those *givens* in my life. Our coach's name was Coach Ray, just like the tryout sign had said. And when I got to the practice field, I saw *him* right away. He also taught freshman gym, so I definitely had seen him around before. He was smiling when we all arrived, and that made me feel good. And so many guys turned up for that first practice. Big guys, small guys, guys who had played before, and guys who hadn't. No girls showed up—they didn't allow that back *then*. They do *now*, and I'm glad of that. A few of the guys brought their own gloves and their own bats, but most of them, like me, simply brought themselves. That first practice was on a Friday which might have been for me lucky or unlucky, because if you remember, *I* was born on a Friday, some fifteen years or so earlier. To tell you the truth, I didn't know baseball from the square side of our farm. I knew you were supposed to hit the ball as far as you could, and you were supposed to catch the ball if it just happened to come your way. That was the extent of my knowledge about the game they called baseball. I didn't even collect baseball cards like other kids did.

But *that sign* outside of the principal's office that Friday with Coach Ray's name on it? For whatever reason, fate or the like, for me was to be the world's biggest magnet. It pulled at me, and tugged at me and I had no control. Nor did I want any. Lomar High baseball and I from that Friday on were just meant to be. I made the team, was a starter, and played centerfield. And from my freshman year on, I broke almost every existing school baseball record. I stole more bases, hit more home runs, and played more consecutive innings. I never, *ever* missed a Lomar High baseball game. Just like I never ever missed a single day of school. But I worked hard at it. If you have to know, I lived, ate, and breathed baseball. I still did all of my chores and didn't ignore my family and friends. I was still totally me, but I simply added a few more hours a day for the sport that I learned to love so much.

And Coach Ray? He taught me much more than just baseball. *Not* that he took over where my dad left off—no one, and I mean *no one*, could ever replace my dad. Coach Ray was just Coach Ray. Baseball to him was just like life. He guided me on all of the right paths—how to be a good sport even in defeat, how to have no ego, how to be gracious. Winning surely *wasn't* everything to Coach Ray. In fact he often told us that sometimes you might even win by first losing. We all loved him! The players, the parents, and even the players and the coaches from competing teams. How could they not?

Of course I remember, in detail, my very first high school baseball game. I started in centerfield. I was *so* nervous! But the coach was right there and gave me this huge hug and this thumbs up, and I just knew, right there and right then, that no matter what, everything just had to turn out okay.

That first game was against a school called Southgate. And there *I* was, Walt Stillman, in the outfield, I guess pretending as hard as I could to know what I was doing. Coach Ray had always told us that you are who you pretend to be. So *that day*, that exact time, I really was convinced that I was the great Mickey Mantel. Of course I was also praying that no one would hit the ball anywhere even near me. But for sure, that simply wasn't to be possible, as Southgate had some serious power hitters. The number on my Lomar jersey was eleven. And it stayed that way for all of my four years. My whole family was in the stands for that first home game, I mean *everyone*! My mom and dad, a few aunts and uncles, of course my cigar-smoking uncle Karl with a K, and even Weepy, my dog.

Now, looking back, I'm sort of glad *it* happened, what of course *eventually* had to happen. I'm glad that it happened in my *very first* game if it had to happen anytime at all. I guess it was nothing unusual for the seasoned guys, but catching my very first ball hit to center-field was, for me, an event. As years were to fly by, there were to be hundreds, but *this one* was to be, for me, the best. The hitter's name was Meekin, and his ball soared far and high. It was like some small white meteor blasting through the sky, and for me, catching it almost meant the saving of our beloved planet Earth. I stopped…I turned…I lurched…I stumbled…I ran…I stretched—and I caught it. I caught Mr. Meekin's high-powered white meteor. *Thud*, was the sound, right in the middle of my glove. It sounded so good. It was one of those *nice* noises that I was to get used to over the next four years.

The other team started to take the field, but I was sort of frozen in the exact spot where I had caught the fly ball. One of my teammates yelled to me, "Good catch, Walt!" and that sort of broke me out of the wonderful trance that I was stuck in. And when I got to our dugout, Coach Ray gave me this *double* thumbs up. That was to be *our* sign from then on between coach and me.

In the midst of all my freshman year growing up, my dad got me my very own first baseball glove. But it was *how* he gave it to me that I'll always remember. It was right after that first game with Southgate. We were home at our farm and my mom asked me to take out the trash. That seemed a bit strange, because there wasn't a whole heck of a lot of trash, and she sort of ignored the whole fact of my very first baseball game. But when it came to my folks, I never asked any questions—I just lovingly did. So I went to the kitchen, grabbed the *half-*full bag of trash, and walked it around back, like I always did. All the time, my dad had his face buried in our local newspaper. Something was up, but I had *no* idea!

As soon as I got to the exact spot where I always put the trash, there *it* was! To me, *it* almost glowed. For sure it was the most beautiful baseball glove that was ever ever made. There was a big green bow tied to it and a note with my mom's handwriting that read, "This is our Walt's glove." I still have the glove and I still have that note in this special place for my special things.

Hey, I realize that to kids *today*, a baseball glove is *not* the most earth-shattering of gifts. Kids today seem to expect so much more. Or maybe I'm wrong. But I do know, with some certainty, that there is a big difference, between kids today and kids when I was growing up. I remember my first bike. I had the same bike for ten years. I polished it, I took care of it, and I knew, I just knew, that one bike was to be my only wheels for a long long time. Hey, I'm *not* knocking today's kids. They surely have it better than I did, but then again, I surely had it better than the kids growing up before me.

But getting back to my very first glove and baseball. I guess besides some personal stuff that I achieved, it was something simply connected to the game that I loved so much. The bases, the bleachers, the fans, the sounds, the smells, the umpires—the *everything*. I realized that the students and the teachers liked what I did on the baseball field, and that was nice and I appreciated that, but *to me*, it surely *wasn't* about *that*. It was about trying to carry out some great tradition of the players before me—it was about decency and caring and fair play. It didn't matter to me that I started, and it didn't matter that I had broken some existing records. What mattered to me was that I was simply there, good, bad, or indifferent. Call me Mr. Square, but that's just the way I felt—and still do. I was a part of something, something American, and I simply was grateful for the chance.

Chapter IV

A Girl Named Molly

However something *else* happened to me in that, my freshman year at Lomar High. I met my Molly. *Baseball* was to change my life, but *Molly* was to alter my very soul forever and ever. She wasn't a cheerleader, not that cheerleaders weren't nice—she just was *Molly*. She was more than beautiful. Her hair was brown with tints of gold. Her eyes were chocolatey brown. And her nose and teeth, to me, were almost perfect. One of her teeth had this unique blue tint, and from the very beginning I was convinced that she was a blue angel. Of course we had our share of squabbles and disagreements, as the usual teens do, but there was this invisible golden glue that actually cemented us together. A golden glue that always made everything just right. Our very first meeting, just like with Coach Ray, is still very alive in my mind. There she was, sitting with all of her friends at lunchtime in the school cafeteria. She was so different, so beautifully different. My love for her, happened *right there*, *right then*, right in our high school cafeteria. There was a pure niceness that seemed to surround her, that set her apart from anyone else, except my parents, whom I had met thus far in my young life.

I pretended that I *couldn't* find an empty table to sit at and just *happened* to land at her table. I wondered if she even noticed me, or if she even cared that I was the same Walt Stillman who was making Lomar baseball history. I had already played five varsity games as a freshman, and to tell you the truth, I guess I had a *teeny* ego, although Coach Ray warned against it and although my folks raised me not to have one.

Anyway, as I found out years later, *yes* she noticed me, and *yes* she knew that I was a baseball jock. That day of our first meeting, Molly made me feel totally at ease. She had such a nice smile and such a warm voice. Right smack from the first meeting she seemed to be different than most of the other human race. Not that I'm knocking us humans—I'm not. We all have our ups and downs. Molly just seemed to be *unpolluted*—that's my opinion. And though opinions do vary, I am at least entitled to have one. When I sat at their lunch table that day, I tried *not* to listen. And that was hard, as they were all talking about this one girl, who *didn't* make their sorority. Unlike me *not* being in a fraternity, Molly *did* pledge a popular sorority. I think it was call Pegs. It's hard to remember now. But I think that's what it was called. The girl they were talking about? Her name was Lucy. *That* I do remember. And they were really laughing and making fun of her—kids can be so cruel, so, so cruel.

At the table that day, it bothered me that they were doing that. I wasn't raised to do things like that. But I kept quiet. I didn't say a word, but Molly, in her own Molly way, totally stuck up for Lucy. And the other girls stopped laughing and making fun of her. Of course, I didn't really know Molly, even her last name, but to tell you the gospel, for whatever fate or reasons, from that moment on, in my heart anyway, she became *my Molly*. She didn't know, of course, what I called her and what I immediately thought of her, but if I had anything to do with it, it was to be me and my Molly from that moment on.

As time went by, I called her *Moll*. We were, in and out of school, absolutely inseparable. I just loved being with her. Both of our families warned us to go slow, even to date others. But that just *wasn't* going to happen. From that first moment on, there was something between us that transcended even time. There was to be no dating of others for me or for Moll. There just was to be an inseparable *us*. It's true that I didn't miss a single day of school, and it's also true that I excelled at baseball, *but* my grades surely *didn't* set the world on fire. Moll's did—she never even got a B, all As, every time, from her freshman year on. And everybody loved her. Me, her family, the teachers—everybody.

I had *baseball* and Moll had *art*. She could draw or sketch anything. In my eyes, she was a real Mrs. di Vinci. And she liked to vacuum. I know that sounds awfully strange, but she did. Give my Moll a vacuum and a rug and she could surely work miracles. She used to tell me that she loved the way the rug smelled and looked when she was all done "raking." And I'd have to tell you that it did look and smell great when she was all done—almost like brand-new. We were also slowly becoming each other's best friend. I would rather hang out with her than my baseball pals, even though I liked them a lot. And she would rather hang out with me than her sorority sisters, even thought she liked them a lot. Our mutual friends just seemed to understand that it was just the way that it was to be. We were best friends, boyfriend and girlfriend, and inseparable. But a *healthy* inseparable, if you know what I mean. We *did* take it slow like our folks suggested, but we simply never got tired of being with each other. We truly meshed. I'm not and never was a big reader of Shakespeare, so I can't vouch for Romeo and Juliet, but it was obvious to us that for sure we were each other's missing link, each other's perfect other half.

As time went by and life became real, Moll and I endured—as you'll find out from me later—many many hardships. But the special golden glue that bound us as one, only got stronger. There *was* back then and *still exists* right now this special tree on our Stillman Farm. A gnarled, knotted oak tree that in one *carved word* says it all about me and my Moll. The twisters and dust storms never even dented it, and even my dog Weepy never used it. Moll and I had carved a heart with our initials also carved smack in the heart's center, and the one word carved underneath it all was "Forever"! We *didn't* put our heart or our initials or our word forever, in the tree's *middle*. We never would have hurt anything. It is at the tree's bottom, and even now, after all these years and after all that has happened, once in a while I will visit, sit by it, and oh, how I remember.

Chapter V

We Slowly Become One

Moll's parents were just like mine. Kansians, hard-working and honest people. And also like my folks, though with the usual warnings, they backed us both all the way. However I must tell you, they *didn't* like it when I called her *Moll*. They always nicely reminded me that her birth name was Molly Francis, and "Moll" was just *not* in the woodwork. And I sincerely tried when I was around *them* to honor their request, but all other times the shorter *Moll*, just seemed to slide out.

I'm glad I've told you that we surely had our fair share of high school squabbles and tiffs. And like all red-blooded teenagers, Kansian or any *ian*, we also had our fair share of screw-ups. I remember one in particular time that we royally and horribly screwed up. It was all about what we decided to do *after* our junior prom. Moll had decided, all on her own, that we—she and I—were going to fly all the way to New York for thirty hours. *She* was so serious about it and because of that, *I* became serious about it, too. We were determined to see the famed Empire State building and walk through that Central Park. It was to be *our* secret, *our* planning, *our* trip. That's what Moll wanted and, of course, I obliged. Hey, we had a ball. Two Kansians— two Kansians in love—two Kansians in love in the Big Apple—it couldn't get better than that.

But we *hadn't* thought enough. Our parents, all four, were frantic and berserk with worry. Still being kids in grown-up bodies, we just *hadn't* thought of the consequences. I mean, we had thought before about not hurting a tree by cutting it in the middle, but we *hadn't*

18

thought about our parents for those thirty hours. That was wrong as a teen, and I'd still be wrong now in my fifties. We should never have a good time at the bad expense of another living creature. And we should never, and I mean never, take advantage of our loved ones. And we did, after our junior prom. We took advantage of our parents. We didn't mean to, but we did nonetheless. We made a pact, right at that point in our young lives, to never do anything stupid like that ever again.

Oh, by the way, Moll won Miss Junior Prom. And believe me there *wasn't* a cocky bone in her body. I know for a fact, that she didn't even vote for herself. I did, but she didn't. I'm sure my Moll had faults and flaws, but looking back now, *I* can't find any. Nor do *I* want to. Like I've told you, she was the closest thing to perfect that perfect will ever be. That's just the way I'll always feel.

It was the two of us together through all of Lomar High, and it was the two of us together as graduation crept right up upon us. There was a possibility that I might get a small college baseball scholarship, but things on our farm *weren't* going so great, and I just felt that it was my time to step up to the plate to help my folks. They argued against it, but I had my mind made up—I was going to get a paying job to take some of the money pressure off two people who had given me so very very much. My Moll agreed, as she knew my heart, and she herself went on to a *local* art college. She, too, wanted to stay close to her family, to me, and to my family.

Chapter VI

High School Ends

Perhaps I'll always miss not formally going to college or maybe I won't, or just maybe I'll go to college in my *next* life go around. Like I told you, my folks didn't ask me, but they were in money trouble on our farm, and they and Moll were my two priorities. Hey, I know that college is a blast. I'm sure that I would have liked it. But, like I just said, perhaps in my *next go around.* I'm surely not one to just believe in *only* what I can see, feel, or touch. And if I had to bet, I'd bet that there's a lot of strange and unexplainable things that occur in this thing we call our universe, things such as our *next go around!*

Well, I never ever made it to college after high school or after anything. I landed a job where the pay was steady and the benefits were a-okay. It took a year or two after high school, as this job that I wanted had somewhat of a waiting list, but my Moll insisted that good things come to those who wait. And as usual, she was right. I worked at Lomar Electric company from about my twentieth year till about what happened to me happened, long about my thirty-fourth year. It wasn't a flashy job, or a fancy job, my very first job at the electric company. It was simply meat and potatoes, a steady and trustworthy job. And at that exact time, for helping out my folks, that's all that I needed and that's all that I wanted.

Hey, as all good stories go, I started at Lomar Electric at the *bottom*—and I mean the *very* bottom. In the company's basement stockroom, my job back then was sort of a glorified "put-things-away man," and "keep-track-of-things man." Of course, I was *not* in charge of anyone or anything. I was a proud assistant to the assistant, and *that* job and *that* title were fine by me. Three of us worked in the company's basement stockroom back then—the boss, Mr. Terrington; Paul, the first assistant; and me. I called our boss "Mr. T" and he was the greatest of greats. Not even a speck of ego or meanness in him. I was blessed by Coach Ray in high school and Mr. T. thereafter.

Mr. T. had the purest of pure blue eyes and pointy ears like Mr. Spock on that ol' TV show about a spaceship. He was the greatest of bosses, and through thick or thin, as our boss, he always stood up for Paul and for me.

I remember one day back then that Mr. T. showed Paul and me *really* what he was all about. Paul and I were talking a lot on this one particular day. I was telling him all about my high school baseball. Paul wasn't much of an athlete, but I guess he began enjoying it a little by way of my stories. There we were this one particular day, our feet all propped up and our hands locked behind our necks like we were the big executives. And right there and right then, the big boss of the whole tootin-fruiten electric company walked on in—I mean *thee* boss of the whole shootin' match. I still remember exactly what he said to us both that day: "Gentlemen, where is Mr. Terrington?" and then quickly, briefly, just he as he had arrived, he also left. Thinking back now, I'm sure that Paul must have pooped his draws. And me? For sure I was frozen right there where I sat, legs still propped up and hands still locked behind my neck.

It was just a bit later that our Mr. T. returned to the stockroom. And *we* knew, that *he* knew exactly what had happened. But he was so so cool about it. He quietly explained to us that sometimes shit just happens and we should move past it, learn from it, and surely *don't* waste anymore time worrying about it.

It was a few years later, as I slowly moved up the work ladder at Lomar Electric, that I found out that if it wasn't for Mr. T. that day, our butts were going to be fired. Long live our Mr. T.! Anyway , it was to be about two or so years later that I was to receive my first official promotion—I was to be *first* assistant to Mr. T. Paul *wasn't* demoted—I wouldn't have gone for that. I was simply raised up a bit. I wouldn't have taken a promotion if it was over my pal Paul. I just wouldn't have!

My Moll took me out to celebrate that first promotion. We had Chinese, and she made me this beautiful card with a big cheese drawn on it. She herself was doing great at art college and probably could have handled art college *and* my job if she put her mind to it. She was so capable and so competent—probably could have even played baseball if she set her sight to it.

Anyway, we had a heck of a stockroom crew. We did our jobs but also had fun. Mr. T. made sure of that. Oh, sure, there were days when I daydreamed about a lot of stuff. Like, what if I had gone to college? Or what if I had a shot to try out for the pros in baseball? But I'd have to say, dreams put aside, I truly enjoyed my life, felt real secure at my job, and loved my folks and my Moll so very much. But some of those daydreams back then sure were delicious!

I've told you my parents didn't expect or ask for my help. But from each one of my four weekly paychecks, I'd take a little money out and put it into my dad's favorite tobacco pouch. It was like a ritual, and I *loved* doing it. It just made me feel real good all over to be able to give back even a tiny bit of what they had showered on me. *They* knew that I did it, *I* knew that I did it, and no more words had to be said after that. That's nice to be able to do *that*—you know, to give something to someone, and expect *nothing*, not even a thank you back. The giving itself was all that I wanted. And of course, them receiving it. As the electric company was to have it, and before I turned that fateful age of thirty-four, I was to rise many levels, receive many company awards, get bonuses, and get praise for my work from the higher ups. I was grateful for it all, and I took nothing for granted. I did my job, tried to be as helpful as I could be, and never ever tried to get ahead at someone else's misfortune. A *golden rule*, that I was taught early by my parents, to try my best to live by.

I often think about things like that—like who *really* said "the golden rule" for the first time? Did Moses *really* part the Red Sea? And or? And or? I guess even now at fifty-four, and probably forever and ever, I'll be fascinated by things like that. We may get older and even wrinkle a bit, but we never ever change *everything* about ourselves—never! Some things always stay with us, just right beneath our surface. That's where they live, stay, and from time to time just pop on out. I must say that I do *read* a lot—an awful lot. Maybe it's because I never went to college and in my own small way, I'm trying my best to make up for it. I read anything and everything I can get my hands on— menus, road maps, almanacs, encyclopedias, anything and everything! Sometimes I don't even finish what I start, but at least I'm reading. I truly believe that if you *don't* read, cobwebs will grow and eventually, each and every one of the non-readers will drown in his or her own poopies. I do realize that with all us humans do in the course of a day, it might be difficult to find some extra reading time, but I really think we just have to make some.

Even back in my Lomar baseball days, Coach Ray always stressed to us the importance of reading. He'd bring in books about the history of baseball or the techniques of the game or of some legendary players, and while we did our stretching, we'd read. We'd read to each other, and we'd read to Coach Ray, but we *would* read. The coach thought decency and reading and drinking lots of water were *all* an important mix.

Anyway, I was to work at Lomar Electric from graduating high school or a few years thereafter till what happened to me happened to me at about age thirty-four. I was assistant to the assistant, then first assistant, and finally stockroom full manager. And then, right before it all started to happen to me, I became manager of the whole friggin' company motor pool. From toilet paper to cars, but I loved it all.

Much time also passed in between each promotion and much indeed happened to me in my personal life, like the *Army*! The army came right smack-dab in the middle of everything, and so did *Vietnam*. But I'll get to all of *that* later. *That* I promise!

It's like I told you, I loved my years at Lomar Electric. I watched myself learn and grow. Hey, there are things in this world that I *don't* like, let alone love. I *don't* like phonies! I *don't* like prejudiced people! I *don't* like name callers! I hate the "N" word! Why do people do that? You know—make fun of other people? My parents disliked it a lot, and surely, so do I. We all have two eyes, one head, bones, and blood. We all have had, or have, moms and dads. We all try and breathe on our own. Dammit, just like our forefathers said, we all were created equal. I also *don't* like and never will like people who thrive on other people's illnesses and misfortunes. One of my aunts, Aunt Alice—not on my uncle Karl's side—did just that. Every time someone got really sick or went bankrupt or was going to die, Aunt Alice switched into her battle gear. She was invigorated and at her finest. I'm sure she meant well, but damn, I surely didn't like it.

Of course, besides my Moll, and my parents and my job, I also had other major *likes*—yes, besides baseball. I liked the whole process of getting up, going to work, putting in an honest day's work, and later getting paid for it. I really like a roaring fire on a bitter cold day. I like a nice comfy bed to sleep in when I'm dogged and flat exhausted. I like *old* songs from *my* generation. I like decency and I like honor. I like taking long walks around our Stillman Farm back then and even now. I guess each of us has their own set of likes and dislikes. And that's probably okay.

Anyway, I loved my years working at Lomar Electric before and after my army stint and before and after Vietnam. I wish all people from all over could like what they do even a teeny bit or as much as I did. Anyway, I was truly grateful for being able to simply do what I truly enjoyed doing. I was grateful and I was appreciative.

Chapter VII

Uncle Sam Called Me

From graduating high school till that six month period in my thirty-fourth year, about seventeen or so years must have passed. I guess about *that* many. And it was true that working at Lomar Electric in one capacity or another accounted for a lot of those seventeen years. But *two other* events also happened during that time frame which, for the purpose of my story to you, are very very important—going in the army and marrying my Molly. And both need some serious talking about.

I surely *wasn't* drafted, although not being in college, I probably would have been. I enlisted! Or as they called it, I volunteered! The army, like baseball, to me was American, and I just *couldn't* ignore it. My folks were scared; Molly was supportive; my job at Lomar was very understanding; and Vietnam, was Vietnam. It was in the *sixties* and things were heating up nicely over there. For me, going in the army *wasn't* an *option*, it was an honorable *must*. The bosses at work told me that they were proud of me, and I could count on them *after* my Army hitch. *That* made me feel real good. They were proud of me for enlisting, and I guess my folks were, too—but they were, like all parents at *that* time, scared. *I* was *all* they had. I was twentyish or thereabouts and had been out of high school for about five or so years.

So, I took a leave from work, said goodbye to my Moll and my parents, took one last walk around our farm, and began my three years of active duty, everyone's favorite uncle, *Uncle Sam*. My first even *hint* of army life began on my bus ride to the place where I was to do my eight weeks of basic training. And that was to be at Fort Polk in the

good ol' state of Loui... ...
Kansas was once a pa... ...
and the fort *wasn't* to ...

On the bus ride t...
of us brand-new, shinn...
long ago. We were al'...
and some enlisted, like n... ...ryone was dressed in different civilian
clothes with different haircuts and different expectations. That was all
to change. There'd be *one* haircut and *one* expectation—the *army* haircut and the *army* expectation. But I understood and I guess I still do.
They had their job to do, and we recruits had ours.

I remember now, it was the month of October, right around
Halloween time. We always made a big howdy-do about Halloween
at our Stillman Farm, but *this* Halloween, I *wasn't* to be there. The
guy driving the bus was in green army clothes with three gold stripes
on his sleeve. I found out later *that* was a sergeant. To us *that day* he
could have surely been king. On the bus the that day, I sat with a guy
from the eastern state of New Jersey. The only thing I really had ever
known about *that* state was that it was *close* to New York, the state
Moll and I had visited after that junior prom. His name was Louis,
that guy from New Jersey. He, like me, had enlisted, and he, like me,
had a girlfriend back home. After that bus ride, our paths were to
never cross again.

It took us many bus hours to get to Fort Polk. The sergeant driving let us sing and amuse ourselves. He let us act like *civilians*, I guess,
for the last time. It was obvious that *he* knew exactly what was coming, no one could have prepared *us*—no one. As soon as the bus finally stopped, we were all herded off by a few soldiers with big Smoky
the Bear hats on. They called themselves D.I.'s or drill instructors.
They were screaming at us, pushing us, and shouting orders at us:
"Go here!" "Stand there!" "Chest out!" "Don't eyeball me, boy!"
Suddenly, right there, right fresh off the bus, right at Fort Polk
Louisiana, I knew exactly what all of our *Stillman Farm animals* must
have felt like. Not that we ever ever mistreated a single one—we
didn't—but if I was to survive the army and get a chance to see those
animals again, you can bet your sweet bippie that if I treated them just
okay before, *now* I would treat them absolutely *royally*. That I swore

to, right there, right then, right at that one moment of my life. I'd have to say that the first eight weeks of my army life, or basic training as they call it, was all that you see on TV—climbing, shooting, push ups, and oh-so short haircuts.

There was, of course, some good and, of course, some bad. We did get our army "dogtags" in basic training, and I still have mine today. I never get rid of stuff like that. Like *that note* my parents stuck on my very first baseball glove. I've still got that, too. I told you that, I'm sure. My army dogtags were RA11754228. I'd probably remember that if I lived another fifty four-years or so. There are some things you just never forget—and some you can't wait to forget. I was never that mechanical, except maybe the woodcraft that my dad used to teach me, but I learned real fast how to deal with my army rifle. It was to be called a *weapon*, not a *gun*, and after a while, I would take it all apart and put it all back together very, very quickly.

Anyway, I made it through the eight weeks of basic with flying colors. I was tired, my hair was short, but I was better for it all. I learned there at Fort Polk that anything is possible to a willing mind. I really, to this day, truly believe that my time with Coach Ray and with Mr. T helped prepare me for my army life. My two wonderful parents had given me all the right direction: they were my *watchmakers*, and Coach Ray and Mr. T were to become my *watch cleaners*.

I learned so many *life* lessons also in the army. In basic training, in my company, which was Whiskey company or W company, I had two commanders. One was a captain, the other a first lieutenant. The captain was a real creep—nobody liked him. He went out of his way *not* to be nice. But our lieutenant went out of his way *to be* nice. He made life worth living for us all at "W" company. It's funny, but it seems that when *certain* people get some authority, any authority at all, they go nuts with it and misuse it. They probably weren't ever taught the golden rule. Or they were taught it but took it lightly. Or plain forgot it. I had this buddy back in Lomar I grew up with. He was so nice, but then he became a cop, and all of that power just went to his head. After a few months on the force, nobody liked him. Not even his girlfriend. What I learned in the army was that with authority, niceness *should* follow. If it doesn't, trouble will come. Hey, there *are* people in authority who *are* nice, like a Coach Ray, or Mr. T. or my army lieutenant.

to do things that I normally wouldn't have, and I probably was in the best shape of my entire life. I was also serving my country and that alone was the biggest of ups for me. Like I said, the *worst* and the *best* of times.

By the time basic training was over, I had made the rank of PFC—one upside down triangle—or private first class. I was proud of myself because I did it the proper way, with grit and determination. But more important than anything was that at the end of basic, we were all entitled to our *first weekend pass*. I was heading back to Lomar. I was going back to see my loved ones. I desperately needed that.

Chapter VIII

That First Army Pass

I guess I had left for the army in a hurry. I just had to do it *that* way or maybe I wouldn't have done it at all. When I left, it was October, Halloween, and that first weekend pass was December, Christmas! It was so good to be bussing back to Lomar. The bus ride home was so much different then the bus ride there. I was an *insider* now, not an outsider to the army. I had surely in those first eight weeks paid my dues. I got tears in my eyes as I got my first view of our Stillman silo. I saw it right from my bus window. Everything inside me was thumping and pumping. It was so good to be home, and at Christmas time, in my army greens, with my bold red and gold, PFC patch. Everybody was there to greet me when I got off the bus—my folks, Moll's folks, and of course my Moll. Weepy my dog was no longer with us.

That first twenty-four hours, I crammed everything in and then some. I saw some relatives and made it a point to see some old friends. I spent as much quality time as I could with my folks, given I only had just a short weekend pass, just a few short days by the time the bus had dropped me off. So when the sacred hour came that I was to be *alone* with Molly, everybody, including her parents, totally understood. I guess it was one of those velvety givens. By then, we had gone together from our freshman year in high school on. It seemed an eternity. Oh, how we loved each other.

From Fort Polk, we had written and planned our weekend aloneness together. This was to be our *complete* first time. We had thought to save that *special time* for marriage, but that just *wasn't* going to be.

It was to be that Saturday of my first army weekend pass. I had reserved a room at a local quaint inn far enough away, but close enough if we really needed anything. My dad had lent me his car, as I had sold mine right before the army. It was Christmas, I was home for the weekend, I was with the girl of my dreams. Oh, was it great. I remember it now, like it was only yesterday.

Molly looked so beautiful. Her hair *now* was more blonde than brown, but her eyes were still chocolatey. She was still my blue angel. That night she wore a black velvet backless dress. She knew that I would love it. And her earrings were two tiny shiny pearls. Our room at the inn was great! It had a hot tub, a fireplace, and even a little ice box, if we needed. Moll had brought a radio and put it on the "oldies" channel. Everything was perfect! And what happened *next* was also perfect. In fact, it was mind boggling. No one or nothing could have prepared us for it. It just sort of seeped out like lava from a sleeping volcano.

As I look back now over all these years, I guess we both must have been scared—scared and tempted and very, very excited. To me, Molly was the very essence of a woman—how she looked, how she spoke, how she walked, how she simply carried herself. I'll never forget her perfume that night. She smelled so good. It was called "White Shoulders." There are *two* smells that I'll never ever forget. The smell of my dad's favorite pipe, and the smell of my Molly that Saturday night so long ago now, in our lives.

The girl I had met so many years before in our high school cafeteria was now the most beautiful of young ladies. Her hair smelt of lilacs, and she always got embarrassed when I told her how beautiful she was. From the very beginning with my Moll, she made me feel that if she was around, I would always be okay. She always, from the first time we met, was my other half. There weren't many things that she *didn't* like. Oh, okay, she didn't like to wear hats, but she *did* it for me. And she didn't really like her *middle* name of Francis, but *I* did, so she went along. Hey, we were our own people, had our own flaws, had our own a lot of things, but there was a *we* about us that just couldn't be denied.

Like I said, it *was* mind boggling what did come next that night, so many years ago. I don't know *why* I brought a black blindfold with me that night. I guess I will never know why. But then again, all the Ys are crooked letters anyway. Maybe it wasn't a blindfold, maybe it wanted to be a HIM and Molly to be a HER.

I remember, even now, so many years later, I was breathing so heavily as I put the blindfold on her. At first she seemed inquisitive, curious, but once I took control, she was quiet and oh, so excited. She had goosebumps all over, and my whole soul was racing out of my body. I slowly took her velvet dress off. *A goddess* with a blindfold on stood totally naked before me. We made love that first night as if the planets had actually stopped in their orbit. *Where* had I , Walt Stillman, gotten the idea from? I didn't know! I guess I still don't! But what I *do* know, is that my Moll *inspired* it! Only *she* could have!

That, our first night, as we mutually touched and grunted and squirmed and became primitive partners was a symbol for what to us was to become a way of life. We had entered into a world, a sacred world, where few go. But we were together in this world, so for us it was and remained, pure ecstasy. We were, from *that* night on, forever linked, not only as Molly and Walt, but also as HIM and as HER. I'd wish on all couples in love *that truth*, that sexual truth, that Moll and I shared. The truth to be ourselves, where we *didn't* have to cheat, we could just be ourselves with each other. That truth worked for us, and for the next so many years together we were almost *contagious*. A look, a gesture, a smell, even a hint, and those two primitive beings, *HIM* and *HER*, just seeped and oozed out of us. We had no control, and surely we didn't want any. I realize that later in my life, a few years down the road, things would come screeching to a horrible and terrible halt, but there were some things *before* that, that I wouldn't have changed or given up for anything—such as that army weekend pass and that volcanic *discovery* that Moll inspired and that I explored. I'm truly proud that I was in the army. And proud later that I fought in Vietnam. Proud for myself and proud for any kids Moll and I were to bring into this world as American kids. I *still* know the Pledge of Allegiance by heart, and every time I say it or hear it, I feel especially good for the small part I played in helping keep it alive.

Chapter IX

After That Weekend Pass

When I returned to Fort Polk, after that incredible and sacred weekend back in Lomar, it was for another eight weeks of training. This time they called it AIT, or advanced infantry training. And once again for the best and for the worst. For sure, not an eight-week walk in the park, but then again, we had to be ready, just in case we got *those* orders. Basic training was to get you generally ready, AIT was more specific. None of it was for the faint of heart, but I understood. We were all getting ready, just in case. So many of the guys on a daily basis were getting their orders for Vietnam or "The Big Pond," as we all called it. It wasn't a question of who *did*, it was more of a question, of who *didn't*.

We generally got our 'Nam orders at mail call—surprise, surprise! The big joke was when the company mail clerk would say, "Have I got a letter for you," then he'd hand you your orders. This mail guy was, to us all, a real important person. He'd make us smile when we got all those nice letters and packages, and he'd put us in a stooper, if we got Jack squat. And he'd put us in *that* mood if we got *those* Vietnam orders. I can't remember now our mail guy's name, but I sure can remember his face. Hey, in those army days, getting mail and visiting our mail clerk, was the high point of the day.

Every guy would handle it differently. I had my own *mail ritual*. I'd get it in the morning, stick it on my bunk with the tight green army blanket, and I *wouldn't* go near it until my whole day was over with—chow, shower, everything. Then and only then would I open my mail Hey, looking back now, it's amazing how such a simple thing like opening a letter could take on such significant meaning. But to us in the midst of it back then, opening our mail was not such a simple thing—not a simple thing at all. Or maybe it's all a part of being human. I guess, until we lose it, we take some simple things totally for granted—like maybe breathing. In my army days, Moll and my folks never let me down when it came to letters or packages. I can't tell you just how good it made me feel at mail call to hear, "Another letter, another package for Stillman." They could tease me or laugh at me, but nothing could tarnish *that* letter or *that* package at *that* hour on *that* day.

I learned a lot about a lot in basic and AIT at Fort Polk. To this day, if I see a pair of shoes *not* lined up or I see a wrinkle in my blanket, I *just have* to fix it—I just sort of have to. I guess it's an obsession, but a nice obsession, if you ask me. I felt good about serving my country. Like I said before, one day my kids would be proud of me, if I had any. And I did. Down the road, I was to have two wonderful kids.

Our America is a great place. Sure, we have Disney World and fast food and Johnny Carson and pizza, but other countries have them, too, or something similar. What we Americans have that no one else has, is our American history. The very *stuff* and the very *earth* of what makes us who we are. The very stuff that makes the Pledge of Allegiance or the Star Spangled Banner exactly what it is supposed to be. Hey, I'm *not* saying that we Americans are even near perfect. For sure we're not. We have our fair share of murders, creeps, bigots, and the like. But in the long haul of things, as our century comes to an end, being an American citizen is *not* such a bad thing to be.

Chapter X

Orders for Nam

As the world spun, it was only inevitable that *I* too, was to get my orders for "The Big Pond." In fact, I was sure that I would, and *I did*! I was still at Fort Polk, and I guess I had been there for almost *two* years, maybe a little less. I had a year or so of army time left, so if they were gonna get me, it would have been right about smack-dab, just when they did. *Our* mailman had changed: in fact he, too, was sent over, but we still had our mail call procedure. Some things *never* really change.

It was on an early mail call in the month of November. It wasn't a special morning, just a simple morning morning. Thanksgiving time was almost around the corner. I knew when I felt it, the letter that is, exactly *what* it was. I *didn't* have to put it on my bunk and I *didn't* have to wait until later to open it. It was to be the Big Letter For Thee Big Pond. The one we always all thought about, the one that *I knew* that one day I would *surely* get. I guess I was sort of numb—numb and excited all at that same time. Numb just because, and excited because the waiting was finally over and because of all that I thought was to come.

The Army was to provide us with *two* things before actually going. One was a well-needed and well-deserved thirty day leave at home with our loved ones; the other, a special course to help us know what Vietnam was *really* to be all about. Anyway, I took my thirty-day leave, of course, with all of my loved ones back in Lomar. In the past two years since that first weekend pass, I had been home, *only* a few times. There was always this or that creeping up with the army. But *this time*

My gosh, how old was I then? It doesn't really matter. Maybe twenty-four or so. Or twenty-five. I had been in the army by then for a little over two years. But I guess at that point, age or years or seconds didn't really matter. During those thirty days, I did a lot of different things—said some hellos, and bid some goodbyes. And I remember I walked a lot, an awful lot. Moll and I walked *everywhere*. In the hills, around our farm, to our special tree—everywhere, that was important! We walked. And we made love!

Since that first weekend pass two years before, Moll and I *hadn't* been together a whole heck of a lot. The army kept me so busy. And if I did get a chance to go home, so many more people were always around. Being alone was a rare treat. But for sure our seed had been planted, and both of us wrote and talked much, about HIM and about HER. *They* were our own private code words, and once said or once eluded to, they set off an indescribable fire in the pits of both of us. We both yearned for *our way* of making love. We *wanted* to do it again—we *needed* to do it again—we *longed* to do it again. Like I've told you, my Moll always said that good things come to those who wait. And yes, she was indeed right once again.

During those thirty days, we were almost addicted to each other in *that* our secret world. We made each other crazy, but the *great* kind of crazy, if you know what I mean. We couldn't wait to be alone, Moll couldn't wait for me to tell her "our" stories. And when I told them, they always seemed to differ. But each time, they were so so erotic. She was *always* blindfolded in my stories. Perhaps she was kidnapped, or a naughty girl, or, or, or. We were like *the* perfect key in *the* perfect lock. We just jelled, and for us both it was more than intense. It only added to our *normal* time and made us hunger for our *not*-so-normal time. I will never, ever understand why couples who claim that they're in love won't also share their darker side with each other. Perhaps they're afraid, or maybe even embarrassed, but they shouldn't be.

I have a close friend back home who really loves his wife. They have known each other as long as Moll and me and recently got married. My buddy refuses to share his sexual thoughts with his wife, but he shares them, for money, with girls he picks up. I think he's wrong! I shared everything with my Molly. And she with me. Hey, that's my opinion on being in love—sharing and telling and communicating. To me, that's what it's supposed to be all about. But then again, it's just my opinion.

That thirty-day leave was only the first of the *two* things that the army gave us before our final departure for the republic of South Vietnam. The second thing was to be a very special course in what we actually might expect over there. Just basic training and AIT *might* have been enough. But this special course was to be the *cherry* to the sundae. So they sent us to another fort in North Carolina, where we learned about Vietnam terrain, weather, language, customs, and other vital things that we would surely need to survive over there. We learned how to survive with bad water and no water, spoiled food and no food at all. We learned about loneliness and about people over there who were going to pretend to be our friends, but were in fact our enemy. We learned what to say if we were captured—and, of course, what not to say. At that fort in North Carolina, they taught us from A-Z anything and everything that we would have to know, so as to have any chance at all of survival. It was taught to us, by soldiers and officers, who had already actually survived in Vietnam. *Without* that special course, it would have been like learning to dive with a *net* and never any *real* water—almost impossible!

Chapter XI

Going Over

I *left* for Vietnam about two months or so *after* I had received my orders that November day at Fort Polk. That would have been *after* my leave time and *after* my special course. It was *January*! Just like I could have gotten out of the army altogether, I also probably could have gotten out of going to Vietnam. I was from a farm state, I was an only child, an only son, but I didn't! I just couldn't! Since our country's beginning and through all of our country's history there have been those of us who served and those of us who didn't. My parents knew and my Moll knew that I was the kind of a person *who would*. For me, it was just *a because* and I could live with it back then and I can surely still live with it now. I still have all of my Vietnam letters and my medals in the same place where I keep all of my sacred life's memories. I'm not a hero now, and I wasn't a hero back in that January, some thirty years ago. I just did what I believed in and what I could live with for the rest of my life, knowing that I did.

We flew out of California to Vietnam. It was a strange plane and a stranger route. We went here and we went there, we refueled and we stopped here and we stopped there. Before leaving from California, I called one more time back home to Lomar. I spoke to my folks and said goodbye to my Moll, too. I told them all that I'd be back. On the plane over, I truly began to wonder if *that* was a promise I was really about to keep. I sat right next to a guy who was going to Vietnam for the *second* time—he was a "two timer." We talked, of course, as the plane ride was long, and he explained to me very inoffial of fundly that out of every three guys landing, at one time or another *one* would be killed, *one* would be wounded, and one would be screwed up mentally forever. As I was to find out later, he was just about right on target.

Anyway, when our plane first touched down, it was at some Vietnam airstrip. It was hot, real hot, even though it was January. There were planes coming in and planes going out, going home. They called *them* "freedom birds." Where I first landed, it was called a replacement battalion. You'd stay there for only a few days and then get your real orders for your *permanent* station in 'Nam. Like I said, it was hot—real hot—a stinky, headachy kind of hot! They immediately issued me my helmet, flak jacket, and green and black jungle fatigues and boots. Also some food and water containers.

By then, only a few hours had passed, but already any thoughts of TV hero stuff were gone. I was in Vietnam, right smack-dab in the middle, and all I could think of was keeping my promise to my loved ones on that last phone call home from California. I wanted to be a survivor. I wanted to go home in one piece or to go home at all by one year from then. I *didn't* want to die *there*, thousands of miles away from our Stillman farm and my folks and my Moll. I just didn't! I didn't want to be a Vietnam statistic. Hey, I was there and there was no turning back! Nothing, not even that special course, could have *totally* prepared any of us for what we were to do or what we were to see—nothing! There was no *practicing* for Vietnam. There was only 'Nam itself. I was scared. I guess we all were scared, but some hid it well or were just too macho to admit it. *I* was *real* scared. Hey, we joked, we laughed, we told hometown stories, but hovering over everything and everyone was this huge cloud of fear and the usual question we all asked ourselves—*when* will *I* get hit? *When* will *I* get killed? And if we were going to get killed, would it be a terrible kill or an easy kill? In other words, would we die easy or would we die a grueling, painful death, like with a pungi stick stuck through the stomach?

I was only at that replacement battalion for a few hot days before I got my *permanent* orders. I was going to a place called Pleiku. It was way up in the north, and the stories swirled that it *wasn't* the nicest of places in the country to be sent to. I had won the real live booby prize, mentally screwed up for a great many years to come. As years passed, even after I was married with kids, if I heard a car backfire or perhaps a noontime lunch work whistle, it would immediately start memories of noises and alerts and incoming rounds, all from Vietnam in the past. Even now, in my fifties, it still happens to me. Those first few years after, when things like that happened, I was scared, real scared, but now I've learned to let it swirl around inside me, and then I'll get rid of it, as fast as it came—time and age and it was the less of many evils that had happened and that have helped me cope with my 'Nam flashbacks much easier.

Chapter XII

My Nam Home

Pleiku was to be my home away from home in Vietnam. All of my time was to be spent *there*, except for those first few days at that replacement battalion. I lived in a *hootch* above the ground, and between my wall locker and my footlocker, I tried to repeat the comforts of home. I made myself a pretend telephone and a pretend TV—I know that sounds silly, but at the time it made me feel good, and *we all* did silly things over there in Vietnam, silly things perhaps meant to help us all survive.

There were about twenty or so of us in my above-ground hootch shelter, and most of us became very close. There was no color, no religion, just the mix and the batter of what made us all exactly what we were—human beings. We had an alert system where a different color made us respond to how bad we were being attacked. I forget the colors now, but I think red was the worst, and I still remember the shrill sounds the alerts made, no matter what color it was. When I used to hear them, I was scared, real scared—we all were, even the old timers and even the two timers. I wasn't yet married to Moll, and naturally I had no children, but I didn't want to die, at least not die *over there*. Besides the enemy, there were a lot of *other* things we were fighting in Vietnam. The weather, the insects, the terrain—a lot of other things besides the North Vietnamese.

Back home in the States, a lot of folks were calling us horrible names for even being there. That bothered me—it really did. Here we were, giving up our very body parts, and the very people we were fighting for were calling us names. But not all the people. And it was those, for me, who made my being there totally worthwhile. Hey, I could go on and on about my year—well almost a year—over in 'Nam, but that's really *not* why I'm telling you my story. I'm just glad that I went, for a lot of reasons. Reasons *before* I had a wife and kids, and more reasons *after* I had my family.

I missed Lomar *a lot*. I missed it all. There were times alone in my hootch when the lump got so big in my throat that I actually couldn't swallow and the tears that streamed down my cheeks actually stopped me from seeing. And those who say crying is for women, as far as I'm concerned, are all wrong. I don't think in the Garden of Eden, if there really was one, there was intended a certain thing for a man and a certain other thing for a woman. My parents, Melinda and Walter, raised me differently and I'm real glad of that. Thinking that way is just as bad as being prejudiced. That's just the way I feel!

Anyway, when you had about a month or so to go in Vietnam, they called you a "short timer" a name we all grew to love when it became *our* turn to become one. I had mixed feelings when it was my turn to be a short timer. I wanted to go home so bad! I wanted to hug my parents, I wanted to smell my Molly, I wanted to walk around our farm, I wanted no alerts and no incoming sounds—and oh, how I wanted simply a shower, even a cold one. But at the same time, I didn't want to leave with the job not complete, and I didn't want to leave some of my 'Nam buddies behind.

Anyway, a Vietnam tour of duty was only a year. I arrived in January, so my year was to be up in December. When I was that short timer and had only thirty days to go, I made my very own calendar. Each day, I'd X off a day—sometimes I'd cheat and X off *two* days. As my days got down to single numbers, I remember my body began to respond to my anxiousness. It was so hard to sleep. I would have awful nightmares, and I was more nervous than usual on our daily patrols. Like I said, my story to you is *not* about me and Vietnam. But I *couldn't* have left it out either—then you'd *never fully* understand what was to have come later in my life.

Yes I was, like I already told you, wounded over there. In about my third month, a sniper got me on patrol. I felt a sting, I hit the ground, and my green jungle fatigues were suddenly all blood red. I had been helped me that day was more than great. It was his kind attitude that right at that time in my life got me through the fact that I *wasn't* going to die over there, that I *wasn't* going to be a statistic of 'Nam. Everybody called him "Doc," but to me he was Captain Brian. He had jet-black hair, blue eyes, and had a slight problem with his leg from an old motorcycle accident. Maybe he had been shot once too, and that's why he was so kind and compassionate. I swore to myself right there and right then when he was working on me that I'd look him up when we all got back to the States. I haven't yet, and some thirty years have passed, but in this thing they call life, I've learned never to say never. For sure, I will see "Doc" again one day, somehow, some way. I believe that's our destiny.

Chapter XIII

Going Home

It was December and they were flying us back to California, the same place we had come from, one year before. We came back home on that "freedom bird" that we all longed for, and the attitude *returning* was surely, a lot different, than the attitude we had on *coming*. By then I had made sergeant, the same rank as that bus driver, who drove me to Fort Polk some three or so years before. I also was getting out a few months early because of being in 'Nam. Of that, I was really grateful. As our plane circled the airstrip home, we could see Americans on the ground waiting for us to land. They were carrying signs with ugly slogans like "Go back, we don't want you here," horrible, horrible signs. I had heard that some people back home felt like that, but now I was seeing it up front and personal. I was angry and hurt. Who the heck wouldn't be? After all we had all gone through to have to come home to *that*!

I wasn't the *first* American to get off the plane that December day. I was somewhere in the middle. But the minute my feet hit the ground, I, and all the other soldiers before and after me knelt down with pleasure and honor to kiss our American soil. That's something I'll *never* forget doing. Or would ever want to forget. As for the people holding those signs, yes it surely hurt, but like me, I guess they were entitled to their opinion too. I told you before that I love to read almost anything, and two things that have always fascinated me and still do are our Declaration of Independence and our great American Constitution, even though a history buff I'm surely not.

43

Hey, it's documents like them that make our America the greatest of all countries, but it's also documents like them that give the sign holders *the right* to be just that—sign holders.

Anyway, I couldn't wait to get to a pay phone to call home. I tried to call on this satellite thing once from Vietnam, but it didn't take, so the last time I actually *spoke* to my loved ones was on that phone call from California *before* I had left for 'Nam. *This* phone call, like our attitudes coming home, was so much different than my first phone call and my attitude going over. So very much different!

The phone rang twice back in Lomar, and I heard it getting picked up. I heard my father say "Hello," and I said back "Dad!" So Fort Polk, that Vietnam special place in North Carolina, and Vietnam itself were all to be behind me. But I knew better. I knew that they'd always be with me, just like my shoulder scar would for the rest of my days on the planet earth. I knew it then, and I know it more now, and I'm happy and proud that I served my time. If I had to, I'd do it all again in a heartbeat—wound, weather, insects, and all.

Anyway, I spent a few more days in California getting all my army stuff straight. Stuff like dental records, last physical, money exchange, and the like. They gave us a few lectures and showed me a few films on how to adjust to civilian life and then, just as it started, *Sergeant* Walter Stillman, RA11754228, was *civilian* Walter Stillman once again. I decided to take a train home. No more buses, no more planes, for a while if I could help it. Besides, I had never ever been on train. The closest I had come was the electric trains that I had gotten for one Christmas that I liked so much. I would hope that I've been as good a son to my parents as my parents have been great to me. Through all of my very young years, my army years, my middle years, and even in that six-month Murphy's Law period, my parents were always and always behind me. Hey, I was a normal son—I would hope a real good son. That's important to me.

Once, when I was younger, I royally screwed up—oh, did I! My parents were furious and believe me, I did get punished. My folks had gone away, and me and my faithful dog Weepy were all alone. Being normal and of course being young, I invited some of my friends over to our farm. We did everything and then some that we *shouldn't* have. We made such a mess, we got into the liquor cabinet, and we left this grounded. I remember that just like I remember my one and only snakebite and my one and only twister.

Chapter XIV

Going Back to Work

I had worked at Lomar Electric Company for a few years *before* my army stint, so it seemed only fitting and natural to return there *after* Vietnam. I had left on great terms, written some of the bosses from 'Nam, and was pretty much offered my job back upon my return to Lomar. I arrived home, like I said, in December, so Lomar Electric was nice enough to give me Christmas off, and I was to start back in January. To tell you the truth, I could have really used that month off, for a lot of reasons.

I guess I was in my mid-twenties, not that it really mattered. When I was telling you before about some of my likes and dislikes, I hope that I mentioned just how much I like Christmas time, especially Christmas time back on our Stillman Farm. That *one*, back then, was a great Christmas. Perhaps I was being tested for what was to come later in my life or perhaps it was just great for all of the other right reasons. In Kansas, our sunflower state, we *did* get snow. Not as much as Chicago, but just enough perhaps to let us know that Santa just *might* exist. And maybe it gave us a sense of hope that some of the dust storms and some of the twisters could rob us of.

The month of *December* had always been good to me. The month of my very first army weekend pass, and now the same month I came home from Vietnam. We always decorated our farm to the hilt, and *this* December I guess everyone, including myself, went a little bit overboard. And why not? It was Christmas, I had survived, and we were all together again. As I had gotten older, my mom and my dad put most of the Christmas stuff out, but *this* time *I* did more than my fair share. I needed to do something *normal* and putting up our Christmas lights was as normal as it gets.

Anyway, as all good things must end, so too did Christmas, and it was back to work as usual. When I had left for 'Nam, I was first assistant storeroom manager. *Now* after being back only a short time, I was to be promoted to *full* stockroom manager. Mr. T. had retired. It was his time to kick back and fish, and Paul was to be first assistant under me, where I could watch him, love him, and let no harm ever come his way. I didn't think that I could ever be Mr. T., but for darn sure, just like him, I'd protect all those who worked under me.

Having been in the military, I had a certain order and discipline that truly helped me at my job. I guess because I had attained a manager's position at such a young age, there were those *bad guys* at the company who had it out for me, so I just did my job and continued to learn. If I was to succeed or fail, it was going to be because of myself, not because I stepped on someone or hurt someone. I'd never do that—it just *wasn't* a part of my upbringing and it just *wasn't* a part of who I was. I guess there will always be backstabbers. Even Jesus had Judas and Caesar had Brutus. And I'm sure Lomar Electric also had their fair share. But to tell you the truth, that really never bothered me. I just did my job, and I figured that all else would just sort of fall into place. I liked working in any capacity, in the company's stockroom. No one bothered you, and the job itself involved so many different things. And at one time or another, everyone came to the stockroom, so I got a chance to meet so many different people. And because I liked to read on my off time, I read almost everything I could, job related. I wanted to know the why and the how of exactly what I was doing, and if I signed a form, I wanted to know *exactly* what I was signing.

I told you before, my Moll went to an art college nearby. From seventeen on and when I first started at Lomar and while I was in the Army and all through Vietnam, *she* had received her college degree *and* her masters. We were all real proud of her. From that very first day that I met her years and years ago, when she stuck up for that girl Lucy in our high school cafeteria, I totally loved my Molly—there simply was this magic between us. I told you before that she hated her mule, but *I* liked it. I liked it because it belonged to her, and I liked everything and anything that belonged to my Moll. To tell you the absolute truth, I even loved her parents for making her. In fact, I remember I wrote them a letter once and thanked them for bringing my Moll into this world.

Hey, for sure we were a *human* couple. We had our share of tiffs and squabbles, and once I even saw Moll go to the bathroom. But on all of the important stuff, like family, human kindness, and pure decency, we were in complete agreement. That tree of ours? With the heart, our initials, and the word "forever"? I wonder how old it really really is? I know for sure that it *wasn't* there the day that the Earth was formed. So perhaps sometime there after. Anyway, Moll and I basically were two good people. And we tried real hard to have religion and decency in our lives. If you ask me, I *don't* really believe in such a thing as a bad seed. A long time ago that was the name of some scary movie, where this young girl was just born bad. *That's* what I *don't* believe! I believe that upbringing and environment are the real tell tale, and even if a kid is born from two of the world's worst, if adopted by loving and kind parents, he or she, will be just fine. Like those bad guys who killed that Fenton family years ago in Lomar? I absolutely *don't* believe that at the very second of their birth, that at that exact very moment, they were born serial killers. I don't, and I never will believe that!

Chapter XV

Our Wedding

Once I had become the full manager of the stockroom, the *next* thing that was to happen was the fulfillment of a ten-year or so dream—to marry my Moll. We both were in the twenty-seventh or so year of our lives, and about a year or so had passed since Vietnam. I had graduated from high school, waited about two more years to work at Lomar, worked there for perhaps two or so more, went in the army, headed for 'Nam, and was now back at Lomar Electric. So, if years and seconds really matter, which I *don't* believe they do, Moll and I were about in the twenty-seventh or so year of our existence. I do have certain opinions on *important* things, like patriotism, taxes, and marriage. And yes, opinions *do* vary!

Of course you know *my* feelings on being patriotic. For that, for all of *my* reasons, I'm gung-ho all the way. As to taxes, basically I think that they are cruel and barbaric and an actual plague to us Americans. My gosh, you work your guts out, work your fingers till they are raw to the bone. And still, each year, Uncle Sam takes almost half. And then, finally, when you are lowered into the ground, your remaining loved ones have to pay still more. To me, that's just not fair. There should be another way for our government to raise money. There surely should be.

As to my opinion on marriage, if you have been fortunate enough to find your other half, like I did with my Moll, then marriage is perfect, as perfect as perfect could possibly be. Of course there *are* obstacles, as there should be! Marriage is not and shouldn't be this perfect,

.... football field. There leave in the same particular
and gravel and some poopy hidden somewhere under all of that green grass. Hopefully the potholes won't be *that* extreme or *that* severe. And maybe, just *before* a couple gets married, they should be able to push a magic button so as to get a glimpse of all that lies ahead. Hey, if you could see and alter, that would be great, but to see and not to be able to change anything, I just don't know if that magic button would be good or bad. Anyway, what is is, what was was, and what is to be is to be.

We had chosen our lucky month of *December* for our wedding, and it was to be held at our Stillman Farm. Moll wanted it there. My parents were thrilled. I guess as history tells us, we really were just two young kids in grown peoples' bodies. It seemed like yesterday, when my uncle Karl was lifting me high in the air. And only a few years after, that I was peeking at the girls at our local swimming hole. And *now*, in my twenties, getting married to my high school sweetheart. *I* was the full manager of the company stockroom, and *Moll* was teaching art to wonderful kids who happened to be less fortunate mentally or physically than most. As she loved her kids, they loved her back just as much for all the love and magic that she brought to them. They loved their "Miss Molly." That's what they called her.

We were making good money between the two of us, we loved our jobs, and we were terribly in love. I guess we thought that the world was ours for the taking. Potholes? What potholes? Gravel? What gravel? I didn't think we were cocky, I just think that we were in love and the whole world was our oyster.

Like you already know, I was born September 25, 1942, and I was married to my Molly December 9, 1969. Our wedding was almost a storybook wedding. Our four folks decorated our farm both Christmasy and weddingy, if you know what I mean, and if such an animal was to exist. In the days building up to the big day, excitement and anticipation was in the air. Everyone was doing something, everyone was doing their share. I, of course, had no idea exactly *what* I was doing, but I appeared busy and I guess *that's* what mattered. We were going to be man and wife, for better or for worse, until death do us part. And *that*, we surely thought, would be about a zillion or so years down the road. How wrong we were! How terribly and cruelly wrong we were!

Anyway, the smell of Christmas and the smell of wedding was all around our Stillman farm. Moll and I helped pay for everything. Her parents wanted to do it all, but we wanted it all lighter than that or harder on. We both had good paying jobs, so why not help out! That's what family is supposed to be all about. For me, on that December 9th, it wasn't really hard to pick my best man. He had been my best man in one way or another for my entire life. Of course, it was to be *my dad*, Walter Sr.

I remember *when* I asked him and *where*. He was in the den, fiddling with the zipper on one of his farm coats. I guess he got his tailoring skills from my mom's dad, Grandpa Louis. Anyway, I'm sure he had some idea of what I was about to ask him, because he smiled and gave me his full attention. Of course he accepted, and he gave me the kind of a hug that he used to give me after one of my high school baseball games. Besides choosing my best man, no one really gave me too much else to do toward it all. So I went to work, and when I arrived back home, my Moll filled me in on any of the day's details, that she thought I should know.

I know that I've already told you Moll's parents, like mine, were true twentieth-century Kansians. They loved me, and I loved them. Besides having my Moll, they were just two really good people. And I tried as best as I could when we were *all* together, to call her Molly and not just Moll. Everyone had their own special list of people to invite. We wanted to be surrounded by people we loved and who also loved us back. Moll had many of her students there, and of course I had Coach Ray, Paul, and Mr. T. I wish I could have invited some of my Vietnam pals, like Doc, but you lose touch and then life sets in. The word *wife*, to me, was to have a cherished meaning—best friend, sidekick, and my heart's other half. In all the time that I knew my Moll—before marriage, during marriage, and now even thereafter, I *never* ever accepted any other female temptation. That's just the way it was and just the way it still is.

That December 9th of our lives, everything was perfect. Our farm looked the part, the weather was our friend, and love and unity was in the air. The ceremony itself was simple and it surely wasn't long. The man who did it was the same man Moll and I had known religiously since we were both kids. He was the head of our local place of worship and knew us both really well. So his words to us that day came tant and valued words, surely not just words. That day my Moll was radiant. She had to be, to me anyway, the most beautiful bride that ever was. Melinda, my mom, doesn't count, of course—*moms* always have their *own* special category. *I'm* not much of a fashion buff, but that particular day, Moll helped me get all buffed up. Of course I really believe I couldn't have done it without her. I told you before that I really also believed, from the very start, that if I stuck by my Moll, I'd always be really okay. She was to be my good luck charm. No matter what!

Moll wore a traditional white wedding gown. Her hair was down, and she had tiny flowers garnished through it. She looked and smelled so good. We made up our own wedding *vows*, and even now as I tell you my story these many years later, I still remember them word for word. Our *rings* were also simple, not fancy, and that *same word* that was on our tree was also engraved in our rings—*forever*. I still wear my wedding band even now as I tell this story. It's been through a lot, an awful lot, but it will never leave my finger. That's just the way it is.

Moll and I just meshed—like I said before, thee perfect key, to thee perfect lock. We *liked* and *loved* each other! Now, twenty-seven years ago? My goodness, where did all of those seconds go? I never did have a heck of a lot of girl experience. Yes, I had a small crush on Gretchen when I was a wee grasshopper, but after that, baseball star or not, Moll was my *only* gal.

Of course, besides our wedding vows and wedding rings, we also had our own very special wedding *song*. For as long as I could remember, Moll loved this one particular lady singer. My Moll called her "Babs." And wow, could she ever sing! Even in Vietnam we used to hear her belt them out, and we'd remember back home. Moll watched all of her movies and knew by heart all of her songs. And though that very famous "Babs" couldn't actually be with us in person on our December 9th, at least *her song* was—it was called "People." A Fred Astaire I surely am not, but *that day*, with Moll in my arms and dancing to *our song*, I at least *felt* like I was.

Anyway, our wedding day, December 9, 1969, was as perfect as perfect could be. What did we know? How could we possibly know, that in a few short years from then an asteroid was to come smashing thing was for sure—we *weren't* cruising to *New York*. In high school, New York got us into trouble, so we weren't going to get burnt again. And we had a ball—sun, fun, and relaxation. So that was our wedding, and that was our honeymoon. Marrying my Moll was what I had always dreamt about since our first meeting, and being *actually* married was far greater than any of my expectations. Okay, sure, we had our own personalities, our own jobs, our own set of friends, even our own cars, *but* when it came right down to the nitty-gritty, my Moll and I were simply one.

Chapter XVI

A Few Years before Murphy's Law

We really did everything quite normal that other young married couples did. That is, before Murphy's Law hit us like that asteroid a few short years down the road. We worked, we loved, we tried to save some money, and yes, we had kids. I guess *by then* we had both reached the big 3-0. We had our kids almost right away. I was still full stockroom manager, and my Moll was still teaching art at a school to kids a wee bit less able than most.

First we had a girl, and then we had a boy. They were about a year and a half or so apart. We called our two bundles of love, Tara and Chad. I picked Tara's name and Moll picked Chad's. We *didn't* need any missing link to make our marriage great. We surely had each other, but our two bundles of joy surely made the best the bestest, and the loving the lovingest. All of our parents, on both sides, went nuts over Tara and Chad—kids, especially *grandkids*, can do that to adults, you know, especially grandparent adults. For sure I saw my mom and dad do things with my two kids that I never thought that they would or that they could. You know, crawl on the floor, make funny faces, stuff like that. My dad, Walter Sr., even put on funny hats to make his grandkids laugh. Both of my kids loved their mom-mom and their pop-pop.

I never thought that *I* could love anyone, exactly as I loved my Moll, but my love for my two kids was *different*. It was deeply immeasurable and totally unconditional. I truly looked forward to the early mornings right before I went to work. I had about a whole hour

I guess I was like this huge daddy grizzly bear, and my two little ones were my cubs. I was protective, loving, and alert to any danger that might come their way.

It was during *this* time in my life, my early thirties, when Tara and Chad were about three or four or so, that I received my *final* promotion at Lomar Electric. It was right before what was to happen to me, Murphy's Law times a zillion. My promotion came as a complete surprise and out of nowhere. I had worked in the company *stockroom* in one way or another since the very beginning, so when they asked me if I wanted to be the head manager of the company *motor pool*, at first I was shocked. What did *I* know about vehicles besides how to drive them? But the big boss told me that it was *not* about pens or paper or tires or jeeps, it was about knowing how to organize and knowing how to be systematic. I credit the army and my beginning years with Mr. T. for that.

Moll and I discussed it since I'd have to work some Saturdays, but after we mutually hashed it out, I happily accepted my new promotion. The idea of the new challenge excited me, just like baseball and just like Vietnam had done. I didn't know diddlysquat about *them*, either. At the beginning, my lack of mechanical expertise was graciously accepted by all, and everyone there began to slowly show me this and show me that. Paul wasn't there with me, and for that I was sorry, but I surely made it a point to call him in the stockroom where he still worked almost every day. And of course, just like with my baseball, I read everything I could get my hands on concerning motor vehicles like we had at Lomar Electric. I read, and I asked questions, and I read some more. And it all began slowly to come to me. I know it may sound strange, but I had all of my workers treat the company vehicles with TLC—Tender Loving Care. I told you way before, and I'll probably in the future tell you again and again, there are a lot of unusual things in our universe, unexplainable things, so why shouldn't a motor vehicle have feelings? Or have even a mom and a dad! That's just the way that I feel!

Anyway, I guess I was getting older. Maybe thirty-three or thirty-four. I felt it, too. My Moll *never* got older, not to *me* anyway. She was still as beautiful and as vibrant as the day I had met her. And she still always smelled so good. Over the years she changed her perfume, but it seemed that every one she picked was made just for her. Like I told you before, *I* named our daughter Tara, and *Moll* named our son Chad. We had seen this movie, "Gone with the Wind" and the famous plantation there was called just that—Tara. I liked it and Moll liked it. And so it was to be our daughter's name. Moll wanted a strong name for our son, and at first we thought of the name Steele. But after some thought, we decided on Chad. Strong like we wanted, but at the same time, no kids could ever use it to poke fun at him like they might have with the name of Steele. We did things with our two kids that probably our parents *didn't* even do with us. We gave them a certain freedom that by nature of the times, Moll and I didn't get. *I* wasn't allowed to ride or to hunt before about the age of eleven. But we started our kids when they were very, very young. I guess just a difference of ideals and a difference of a changing loosening up. I could go on and on about my thirties, my kids, my new job, but I won't. I've told you all of the important stuff. Moll and I were sure that together, one day in the future, we'd be able to explain to our kids that exact *way* that they had got their two names. But as Murphy's law was to have it, that just wasn't to happen.

Chapter XVII

Murphy's Law

I was about thirty-four when it *all* began to happen. The year was 1976, and it was *not* to be a very good year. We had been married for about seven years, and like I told you, Tara and Chad were threeish or fourish. It was all some twenty years ago now because I am now fifty-four. *It*, like our very famous Kansas dust storms, came abruptly, horribly, and out of nowhere. And like that twister when I was younger, there was to be no warning, no preparation. There was to be no anything! Nothing in this world or any other world, could have prepared me for the grotesque horror and complete devastation that was to soon come my way. It was to be the worst possible earthquake that was to create a *permanent* crack in the center of my very soul. It attacked every fiber of me being a mortal human being. It was as if someone had totally exposed every possible nerve in my entire body and was slowly and methodically poking at each of them with the hottest and sharpest of tiny needles.

It all started with my most incredible son Chad, the youngest, by a year or so, of my two. Moll and I lovingly always called him our *Chadster*. We had known for a day that he just *wasn't* his normal, loving self. His whole body was hot, his tiny head was hurting, and out of nowhere, this red rash started mapping its way across his small body. He was in agony, and we were agonizing along with him. We tried the normal things that good parents try to help their youngsters, but finally and smartly, we took him with us to our family doctor. His name was Doc Cutler, and all in Lomar loved him. He was aged, wise, families, almost forever. After quickly examining Chad, Doc Cutler told us, that it was good that we brought him, and that he had this thing called scarlet fever. However we had caught it in time, and with antibiotics and rest he was sure that our Chadster would be just fine.

But for us and all of humanity, that just *wasn't* to be the case. Our Chad died! At home in his own bed, abruptly, quickly, and hopefully without a drop of pain. He had suddenly stopped breathing, and it was over. I had had the pleasure of his company for only those brief few years. Yes, I had heard him say *"Daddy,"* but I'd never hear him say *Dad*. And what about baseball? And his first date? Oh, what about everything? For me, all was a blur, sort of moving in slow motion. It seemed that that day and the next, everybody in Lomar paid their respects. Coach Ray was there, and of course Paul and Mr. T. My parents and Moll's parents were eternally soiled. Doc Cutler couldn't even speak, but we all knew that it wasn't his or anyone's fault. I was totally and absolutely frozen, and from that moment on my Moll *wasn't* Moll anymore. It was as if someone had reached into her middle and ripped out her very soul, her very stuffings.

At his tiny funeral, our religious leader, the same one who had married us seven years before, tried to explain it all—he tried his very best to put things in perspective. I was *listening*, but I just wasn't *hearing*. For me and Moll, there was to be no explanation, no perspective. We had lost one of our bundles of joy. He was gone, and we were gutted—forever. That was the *first time* in my life when I doubted! And the first time *ever* that I screamed up to an unanswering sky, "Hey, God, are you really really up there?" I was on my knees and that's exactly *how* I yelled it back then. Up until that point in my life, I had only been to *two* funerals. My dog Weepy, and my pop-pop on my dad's side. And back then, they both shook me terribly. I've already told you that back in those days, I truly believed that people you loved simply lived forever and ever.

Anyway, my Chad's funeral was different than the other two that I had seen before. Different than *anything* I had experienced up until then in my life. *How* could God have done this? *Why* would He have done this? I went through some motions—organizing, consoling, and thanking all of those who took the time to pay their respects. I tried so hard to be busy, and then busier. But my Moll, unlike me, *didn't* keep busy. And she *didn't* organize, either, or thank a soul for coming. She just simply was there in body only, mourning, weeping, and occasionally grieving, but my Moll was empty of everything. If I live until I'm 106, I will never forget the day that I buried my tiny son. I was supposed to be his champion—how could I have let any harm come his way? I was his all in the world. I was supposed to protect him from everything and everyone.

Little did I know at the time that my son's death was only the *first* of the *many* things that were to happen to me in that six-month period in the thirty-fourth year of my life. A few weeks after our Chad's death, our Tara began to *stutter*—it was almost all the time and almost uncontrollable. Chad and Tara were very close, so we all thought that her stuttering was due to her brother's death. Moll was still a wife and a mommy as best as she could be, but she was at most only a shell of her former self. She had lost almost twenty pounds, and some of her beautiful hair was beginning to fall out. All of the people in the know told us that both Tara's stuttering and Moll's physical stuff was all due to nerves, that nerves could cause almost anything. Her folks, my folks, and of course me, her Walt, became a constant support team for her. And it was my greatest pleasure because of how much I loved her and how much I wanted her to get back to her old self. When we were awake or asleep, I cared, nurtured, and loved her. And when she smiled, I would always give her one of my old Coach Ray's double thumbs up. Her slightest improvement received the highest praise from me. From my job at the motor pool, I would call to her school just to leave a message with the school's office of how much I loved her. And I knew that she got all of my messages. And when she got home from teaching her kids, I'd have fresh pretty flowers on the table and dinner would be all prepared. She appreciated all that I did, all that we all did, and once in a while, she'd give me a weak but sincere huge hug, just to let me know that I was appreciated. I guess the only real gift that we can truly give is *our time*. Because of that, most of us today surely do not have time. But time, and my love, and my everything, I surely gave willingly and without condition, to my soulmate wife.

Chapter XVIII

Oh, My Moll

I was to *lose my Moll*, fifty-eight days, four hours, and twenty-two minutes after I had buried my Chad. That is exact, and the seconds surely do not matter. Perhaps if there really was an eighth day of the week, then it was on the eighth day.

It all started out as just an ordinary day, as ordinary as ordinary possibly could be having just lost our son and Tara was still having difficulty talking. I had gotten Tara up and had finished my mommy-daddy morning duties. I had headed off to work at the motor pool and Moll had gone to teach art, at her school to her kids. I think she taught the fifth graders. We never used the word handicapped, I've already told you that, it's just that *her* kid's skills were a little *less* than most. She truly loved her kids and they truly loved her. Like I told you before, some had even been at our wedding years before and were now almost little adults. They always called our house and were always around. Her kids loved her, her fellow teachers loved her—what *wasn't* to love? She was kind, appreciative, beautiful, and so understanding of everybody's different needs.

When Moll left for work that day it was, like I said, just an ordinary day. Of course our beautiful Chadster *wasn't* laughing or playing, and our Tara was still stuttering, but Moll and I, tried our best to be upbeat. In the last few days leading up to *that* day, Moll had promised me that she would try her best to eat. I thought perhaps there was to be somewhat of a light in our oh-so-dark tunnel. And she looked so pretty when she left for her school that day. She wore a black long been through so much. His name was Ritchie. He was very, very talented in art, and my Moll often talked about him to me. He was partially deaf from birth and had a very hard time with his basic balance. But he was getting much, much better and was really excelling with his "Miss Molly." His parents had been divorced, and his dad, a long-distance trucker, had a restraining order against him. Sometimes he was physical with Ritchie and his mom and hated the fact that *his* son had to go to what he called a school for *dummys*.

Anyway, about 11 A.M. on *that day* of my life, it all just upped and happened. Just like with my son Chad, there was to be *no* warning, *no* preparation. The truck-driving father with the restraining order against him burst into his son Ritchie's school. He rushed and pushed by everybody on the school's first floor and made his way to the second floor where his son Ritchie was in his art class with *his* "Miss Molly," *my* "Moll." From what I was told later from the parents of the other kids who were actually there that day, Ritchie's dad was angrily angrily waving a gun. And my Moll, to protect her Ritchie, having just recently lost her own son, stepped smack in between Ritchie and his father. She tried to reason and even plead with the angry father, but on *that* day there was to be no reasoning and there was to be no pleading. There was to be only *one* crackling shot, and my Moll, with a single bullet hole straight in her forehead, fell to the classroom floor. And just like that, my Moll was gone.

When I got the phone call from the school principal, a Mrs. Terry, it was about a half hour or so later. She told me that there had been a terrible, terrible accident and that my Moll had been seriously hurt. I remember now my exact feeling back then. I was numb and I was petrified. In my heart, I just knew that it was *much worse* than just a terrible, terrible accident. In my heart I just felt that my Moll was gone. I ran from work at Lomar and in minutes only was at my Moll's school. It seemed to me that almost the whole world was already there. There were people scurrying everywhere, including lots of police. Everything to me in those minutes was in slow motion. I was getting funny looks from a lot of the people, looks that by themselves alone should have told me that it was a lot more, than just a serious accident.

When I finally got to Moll's classroom on the second floor, some lady police sergeant came right up to me. She knew who I was. Everything was already taped off with this yellow-colored wide tape. The lady police sergeant kept talking to me, but I couldn't hear. I squinted and tried to read her lips. I was so nervous that I just *couldn't* hear a thing. I did get from her that my Moll had been shot in the head protecting a little Ritchie, and for the first time, I actually heard *that* word—DEAD! My Moll was indeed gone! Chad, now Molly, this just couldn't be! God? Please make it a terrible, awful mistake, or a terrible, awful dream, or a terrible, awful *something* other than the truth. Let me just wake up and know that the past fifty-eight days really didn't happen.

But it *was* real and it *did* happen. I was *inside* Moll's classroom now with all of the people and with all of that yellow crime scene tape. And my darling was there, too, on the floor, dead. Just like my grandpop on my father's side and just like my dog Weepy. And of course, just like my Chadster. The police lady *didn't* want me to see her, but she or no one could have stopped me. My Moll looked like a wax mannequin sort of arranged on the floor. I wanted to lift her up to take her off the stone-cold classroom floor, but they stopped me. How could this all be happening? I inhaled and Moll exhaled. We were supposed to be one, until death do us part. *I* should have been lying right there with her. They stopped me from lifting her up, but they couldn't stop me from kissing her. And I touched her, too. She was still my Moll and always would be. Could this all be *my* fault? Wasn't *I* supposed to protect her?

Soon they zipped Moll into a black bag and carried her out. I knew that they weren't being cruel or unfeeling, but it all seemed so matter of fact. I mean, she was my wife, my life, my other half. In Vietnam I had seen those black body bags before. I had flashbacks. But this *wasn't* 'Nam, this was my Molly. What the frig was going on? I mean, before going to 'Nam, I had that special course to prepare me. What possible special course could have prepared me for the death of my wife? I was numb to the bone and frozen.

They were sapped, reacting like I was, as mute zombies. We all were all sort of clinging and falsely hoping. Suddenly her dad collapsed. But all the police around us quickly brought him to his feet. Just like Moll and I had physically suffered when we lost our Chad, Moll's parent's aged twenty or thirty years right there in front of me.

As I look back now, I guess I had so many emotions running through me—anger, fear, hate, guilt, all at the same time. But it's been a full twenty years now since I lost my Moll, and I've had no desire even to go on a single date—not one, not any. What I lost that day, to me, *was* and *is* irreplaceable, and to attempt a substitute wouldn't be fair to the lady or indeed fair to myself. In a blink, that says it all.

Anyway, getting back to that horrible day of my life, my own parents were closely by my side. Wherever I walked, they walked; wherever I drifted off to, they drifted off to. They lovingly stuck to me like glue, and as always, I needed that from them. I guess you never get too old to be made to feel safe by your parents. Even today, at fifty-four, I feel loved and safe when I'm with them. I remember back then, in Moll's classroom, I wanted desperately to see *him*, my Moll's assassin. I pierced the crowd of people that day, looking and searching. What would he look like? I remember thinking that. The man who in less than a flash, ripped my heart right out of its casing. I guess I was sort of alive that day, but then again, not really. Hey, I wanted to be violent—I *needed* to be violent. My whole entire life I was the opposite, but then, right then, the golden rule was the furthest thing from my mind. I wanted to kill him with my own hands, and slowly. I wanted to kill him slowly. My Moll probably wouldn't have wanted me to even think like that, but I was. I'm pretty sure that my dad knew exactly what I was thinking because he stuck as close as close could be.

But Moll's killer *wasn't* any longer at the school—or the *accused* killer, as they referred to him. They had already whisked him away to the police station. My folks and Moll's folks shielded me from most of the flashbulbs and from the many, many news people. But I'd have to say that even the news people were kind to me on *that day*. Maybe because most of them there were also from Lomar, where everybody knew everybody, and from where dust storms strike and from where wheat is the big item. But I appreciated the kindness from the paparazzi. They could have made everything even worse if they really wanted to. And any worse, I simply couldn't have taken—not *one more* feather of worse.

Chapter XIX

Burying My Angel

Everything and anything was blurry for me. I had lost my son, my daughter was stuttering terribly, and my Moll—my Moll—was gone forever. That was to be the *second* time in my life that I doubted. I again yelled up to the heavens, "Hey, God, are you really, really up there?" The second time in such a short period of time. First for my Chadster, and now for my Moll. All the same questions came to me— did I do something wrong? Was I being tested? We were all good people, we followed all of the rules, all of the commandments, yet suddenly, out of nowhere, my beautiful son was yanked away, *and* the kindest and most beautiful of all creatures, my Moll, was helplessly and senselessly killed. When our religious leader spoke at Moll's funeral, he spoke about Christ being taken at about the same age, he spoke about a great design, a great purpose. He spoke about the Bible's great book of Job and about Abraham being asked to offer up his only son Isaac. I *did* listen—mutely and like granite, but I *did* listen. But just like at my Chad's funeral, I surely *wasn't* hearing. I was done hearing. I was done believing!

People came from all over for Moll's funeral. People I knew and people I didn't know. I was sure that my Moll would have been happy about all the people who cared enough to come to pay their respects. I heard so many good things about my Moll that day, things that even I didn't know. And through all of my sadness and all of my grief, I was simply proud to have been a part of her life. Her mom and I picked out the outfit that she was to be buried in. It was her favorite and she simply a *Molly outfit*—and yes, it was *long*, as she would have wanted.

Some people say that dead is dead. I always thought that, too. And when my pop-pop on my dad's side up and died, I learned that even good people don't live forever. I guess before Chad and Moll, almost everything about a funeral used to scare me. The words, the smells, the music, the everything. Anyway, for whatever reason or reasons, I *wasn't* scared at my Moll's—gutted, granite, cold, so so sad, but *not* scared. And there was this *glow* about her as she lay there so still, this almost *orange glow* that seemed to make things a bit more tolerable for me. I'm not sure if anyone *else* saw it, I guess I'll never know that, but *I* saw it, and for me, at that moment, that's all that counted. We all put loving things into her casket with her—and pictures. We put in lots and lots of family pictures. Pictures of us *all* together in the better days.

As I look back now *Tara*, only perhaps maybe four at the time, still stuttering, seemed to be my Rock of Gibraltar. It seemed that so much happened, in such a short period of time. But then again, even shorter periods of time, perhaps only seconds, have been responsible for some of the world's most horrific disasters. Some earthquakes last for only seconds, some twisters about the same. And the damage they do is almost eternally irreparable. I often think now, years later, what my Moll would have thought about it all. You know, about everything. Even about that madman, Ritchie's dad, who had ripped her so so young from us all.

I used to love the way she thought. I used to love her femininity. I liked the way she used to put salt and pepper on her food. I used to like when she ordered coffee from a waitress and would tell the waitress that she wanted the coffee intravenously. I must admit that there were times when Moll was at school, and that I stopped home briefly, I actually would smell her clothing, just to inhale *her.*

So what would *she* have thought about it all? I'd guess that she'd probably have forgiven Ritchie's father, and I'd guess that she'd promise to be there, *forever* for Tara and for me, just like our carved tree said. I admired and respected my wife just as much as I loved her. And I'd have given anything to have had her back—anything. Both of my arms and both of my legs, without even a thought. Because like I told even though my Rock of Gibraltar, was still stuttering, a lot—a whole lot. They all called it nerves, and *I* personally was to find out just a short time later just how powerful the mind and nerves can be in screwing us up. I also probably could tell you all of the details of Moll's funeral, but I really don't want to. They played our wedding song by her favorite singer, Babs, at her parent's request, and *that* I will never, ever ever forget.

During that time, or about that time, *I* went through several changes. It just depended on the day and the hour. I was confused, bitter, angry, and of course, how I questioned the person upstairs, if he was really there at all. I guess questions, questions, and tears and more tears. To be really honest, which I just have to be, I was probably even angry at my Moll for protecting little Ritchie to begin with. I hated Ritchie's dad with a passion. I wanted him ripped and torn and quartered by the world's angriest horses. I wanted them to sentence him to be tied to an anthill and to have all of the ants in the universe eat him bit by bit and slowly, very, very slowly. The only other major crime in Lomar's history was the one that I have already told you about—that Fenton family murder. And it's true that that one was premeditated and coldly planned out, and my Moll's wasn't. But her assassin had a gun, the gun was fired, and my Moll was gone forever. *That*, to me, was all that really mattered, and as far as I was concerned, pay he must.

By the time his trial had started, I hadn't changed my mind one iota about what I prayed would happen to the guy who did it. He could have been angrily quartered by those horses or eaten alive by those ants—it didn't matter which. But what *did* matter was that something horrible should befall him. An eye for an eye. That's exactly what I prayed for at the time. The opposite of how I was raised, but *my* truth nonetheless.

The day of his trial, the courtroom was packed. Even his own lawyer knew, I could tell, that there were to be no getting this guy off. It was almost an open-and-shut case, and the police hadn't messed up

Moll on some legal technicality. He just wasn't! When the deputy brought him into the packed courtroom, his feet were shackled together, so he was taking almost baby steps. He was wearing some kind of a suit and some kind of a tie. I was sure that his lawyer had got *it* for him. Everything was quiet. Reporters and photographers were everywhere, but everything was so quiet. My parents and Moll's parents were on either side of me. My Tara was not there, and of *that* I was glad. No more pain for Tara—no more.

His lawyer did all that he was supposed to, but I could tell that the jury wasn't buying any of it. He was found guilty of my Moll's murder, *not* because he intended for it to happen, but simply because he had started a ball in motion and as a result, my Moll was dead. The prosecutor had a special kind of legal name for that kind of a murder, you know, for starting the ball in motion. I forget right now exactly what they called it. What would Moll have wanted to happen to Ritchie's dad? I remember thinking that back then in the courtroom. Knowing my Moll, I'd probably say she would have wanted mercy. Before the judge passed sentence, they asked *him* if there was anything at all that he'd like to say. That's when he turned to us all in the suit that they had bought him and his tie, and he quietly said, "I'm so sorry. I wish I could take back everything about that day. It never would have happened. Please, please, forgive me!" He was almost looking me right in the eyes when he spoke those words. Then he turned back to the judge and slowly bowed his head. He was sentenced to life in prison with the possibility of parole. But it was *what* he said and *how* he said it that finally would stop me from hating. I'd *never* forget, and I'd *never* forgive, but the horrible hate that was consuming me was lessened. The five of us held hands when his sentence was read. They took him away in the same shackles they had brought him in with.

After the sentence, there was to be *no* party and *no* celebration. For a little while, anyway, I kept in touch with Ritchie, the boy my Moll had protected. I just knew she would have wanted that. I guess I was just going through the motions of my everyday life. My Tara gave me somewhat of a reason to exist. If not for her, I just don't know. I had lost my darling son and precious wife in less than sixty days.

Maybe I needed the trial to be still going on. Maybe I wasn't really ready to accept it all. Maybe I surely needed some counseling. But not enough money and not nearly enough time, as I chose to try to counsel myself. All the good wishers told me to plod on, that things would surely get better. I know that they meant well, but goodness gracious, I had just lost my son and my wife. How do you plod on from that? Even a simple cut needs time to heal. And as far as *I* was concerned, what happened to me was six trillion times *worse* than only a simple cut. *Mine* was a cut to the heart, the deepest and worst kind of a cut of all. Anyway, I did try as best as I could to help myself. I even went and got books on grieving. And I did immediately go back to work at Lomar Electric. And for sure as best as I was able, I tried to take care of my remaining Tara.

But something was *all* wrong inside of me. I knew it, and I could smell it, but back then I could do nothing to stop it. I was almost mentally, helplessly paralyzed. And the bills? All those bills kept piling up. I know everyone who sent them to me felt sorry for me, but they were still *my* bills nonetheless. I guess even bill senders have a job to do. Moll had no life insurance, even through her school, and my electric company only had to pay just so much before *I* had to kick back in. Those days, it cost a lot to die and I had *both* Chad and Moll's death to deal with, along with my missing them so terribly terribly much. And for me, being only a simple peon from Lomar, the whole thing was staggering. I wasn't about to ask my folks or Moll's since they already had helped enough, so on my shoulders and my shoulders alone everything fell. Back then, it was such a heavy, heavy burden.

Chapter XX

Murphy's Law Continues

I began, slowly, to do things that I had never, ever done before or even dreamed of doing. Things that were against my very grain or against who I, Walt Stillman, was. I began to miss work or to go to work, but be late, or leave early. In my high school days, remember, it was *me*, Walt Stillman, who never ever missed or was late for a single day of school. And I began to drink. No one in my family did, so for sure it *wasn't* a gene thing. I had gotten a *second* job a few nights a week moonlighting as a bartender to make some extra bill-paying cash, and that's really when my drinking started. The electric company had no rules against holding down a *second* job and for me, it seemed to fit right in. It was at night, after my first job had ended, and I always made certain that Tara was totally cared for.

My drinking began slowly, almost routinely, but it quickly increased at a rapid pace. At first it was beer only, and then shots, and finally anything that had alcohol in it. I guess it's hard, real hard, to admit that you're a drunk. At least for me it was. Everyone was concerned for me, I guess even my Tara, but I was in complete denial. I was denying and boozing, both at the same time. My job as manager of the motor pool was really being affected. I knew that all of the big bosses at the electric company really liked me. And I also knew that they all knew about my Chad and my Molly and they all felt my pain. But my drinking got worse and worse. All of my fellow work people were going out of their way to help me and to cover for me. I was a total mess. I didn't care about my appearance, my performance, or slowly becoming a different person. Not a mean person, just a person I didn't know and a person I didn't like.

Anyway, as it almost had to happen, they laid me off at my job as the manager of Lomar Electrics' motor pool. It hurt me, but I knew that I deserved it. But because of all the other hurt that I had been recently through, the lay off, by comparison, was only like a *spoon* dropping on my toe, certainly not a hammer. And don't get me wrong, I wasn't fired—just laid off. They told me that they were just going to give me some time to regroup. They couldn't pay me, but I *was* to get something. Hey, I deserved it—I brought it all on myself. The day they laid me off, I went to my office to gather all of my personal stuff. It was rough, and I was angry—not at Lomar Electric, but at myself. Everyone there had bent over backwards for me, but after Chad and Molly, nothing much mattered anyway. Tara was still stuttering, I was still drinking and *now*, I was jobless, and all in such a very short period of time. I had lost my identity. I had lost my pride. I was spiraling down this oh-so-dark and endless tunnel.

The day that I got laid off, I almost automatically went to the first bar that I could find. It *wasn't* the bar I was working at part-time. It was just a bar, a simple bar. And I sat and I drank, and I drank, and I drank. I spent money I didn't have. The bartender kept pouring and I kept drinking. There was a pool table with a green top and a jukebox in that bar that day. I remember I felt like a drifter in an old time western movie. But there I was back then on that day and it was really happening. I *wasn't* a western drifter at all, I was *me*, Walt Stillman. On the jukebox was *our* song, "People," by Babs. That was our wedding song and my Moll's funeral song. I put a quarter in and played it, and of course my eyes filled up and my throat got lumpy. The words of that song that day seemed so so important to me.

I listened and I heard, perhaps for the very first time, and I remembered *us*. I listened and I drank some more. Perhaps the bartender should have stopped me, but he didn't. I wasn't dressed very nearly. I had gone to work that day, the day that I was laid off, and like I told you, my appearance didn't really matter to me at all. I hadn't showered for days and I barely combed my hair. I just didn't care.

As I sat there and continued to guzzle, I thought about a lot of different stuff. I thought about *everything*. About my uncle Karl and my childhood. About my snakebite. About that twister when I was younger. About my very first baseball glove. About Coach Ray. About Mr. T. And of course about my Moll and my Tara and my Chad. And about *our tree*, with the word *forever* carved at the bottom, not at the middle. I had by then eternally lost my son and my wife. My daughter was stuttering. I was seriously drinking and I had lost a job I had treasured and labored at since high school. I guess I just wasn't thinking back then *what else* could possibly go wrong or *what else* could possibly happen? How could there be another *what else* at all?

But of course, there was or there were. My drinking affected my driving, and on several different occasions I had received warnings about it from our local police. Warnings only because, like the rest of Lomar, I was still a baseball hero in many people's eyes and also because everyone in Lomar knew about Chad and my Moll. I was being cut major breaks, and looking back now, I was really lucky.

Anyway, a short time after I had lost my job, I was driving home from work at the bar where I worked. The weather was really really bad and it was pouring a good ol' Lomar rainstorm—and, of course, I had been drinking. It all happened so friggin' fast. For whatever reason, my car swerved into an oncoming lane and suddenly I heard this tremendous crash. I had hit another car. And then my car was sliding down the highway, up on one side. When it finally stopped sliding, it seemed that people, glass, and police were everywhere. Was I dead? Was I going to be dead? I remember back then, right at that moment, thinking just that. But I *wasn't* scared. Not at all—not even a wee bit.

When they finally got me out of my car, I was shaky and a bit bloody, but I *wasn't* dead and I wasn't scared. I did hear people whispering that I had been drinking. I also heard them talking about an older man and an older woman who were in the *other* car I had crashed into. The authorities there at the scene insisted that I go on a stretcher, and I didn't argue. There was no argue left in me.

In the ambulance on the way to the hospital, I was all alone except for the ambulance people. I remember they were very kind and very reassuring. And like I said, I wasn't scared at all. The worst that could happen would be that I'd die, and I'd be with my Chad and my Molly. And to me, back then, that might have been a blessing. Everyone knew that I had been drinking. I surely didn't try to hide or deny it. I *did* care about the older man and woman I had crashed into. They had been hurt, but they would survive; of that I was more than grateful. I also found out that like most of us all in Lomar, Kansas, they had worked hard all of their lives and had children and grandchildren of their own. Certainly *not* deserving, at that stage of their lives or any stage, of the hurt and discomfort that my drinking had heaped upon them.

I visited them at the hospital when I was let go. I needed, for my own heart, to apologize to them and to their children. When I visited them, the couple seemed in discomfort, but they did readily accept, my apology. Their children, about my age, were far less forgiving of what I had done to their parents. But I was so glad that I went, notwithstanding the tongue lashing I received at the hospital from their son and from their daughter. Of course as good ol' Murphy's law was to have it, at the exact time of the accident, I hadn't been able to pay my car insurance, so I had none. And I lost my driving license for six months because of my drinking. I truly thought that I had hit rock bottom. My son and my wife were gone forever, my young daughter was suffering terrible from stuttering, I was an absolute drunk, I had lost my job, and finally, cherry to it all, I was in a senseless car accident, had no insurance, and lost my license.

But rock bottom was *yet* to come. Another *what else* was looming overhead, ready to pounce. During all of this, every horror, every second of that six-month period, my family, Moll's family, and my Tara, were *all my* Rocks of Gibraltar. They never stopped loving and supporting me. I just wasn't loving or supporting to myself. It was right then, amidst all of that, that I first started getting my *panic attacks*. Mr. or Mrs. Murphy, the co-owners of Murphy's Law, were really working me over. Things started to happen to me that had never happened before. I'd be sound asleep and out of nowhere, my heart would start to race and I'd be drenched all over in sweat. I actually felt my skin crawling. The only place that I felt safe was in my own bedroom, and personal fortress or haven.

I had never gone for help to my parents before, not through any of that horrible six-month period, but finally I just had to. It got so bad one night, so bad, that they actually, after I called them, took me to the hospital. The same hospital I went to after my car crash. The doctors there took every test known to man because they wanted to be able to rule things in or rule things out. The doctor on duty that night was really patient and quite nice. When all the tests were done, he sat me and my folks down and told us that I *hadn't* had a heart attack. I was having what they call a *panic attack*. I found out later that they can be brought on by many things and can come out of nowhere. And if anyone in the whole world was a prime candidate for one, after all I had been through, it was surely to be me. There were books I could read and medicine I could take, but the cure after everything was said and done had to come from me. So there I was back then, age at thirty-four, with two great kids, the best wife possible, a job that I loved, and suddenly, in a flash, like that long-ago great twister, it was *all* gone. And I was a drunk, had no license, and was getting panic attacks so severe that they shook my very skeleton. But why? Why out of all of our billions of people, why me?

Chapter XXI

Answer to Questions

I surely knew that I couldn't go on as I was. But I didn't know *what* to do or *who* to turn to. I couldn't ask my folks anymore, I just couldn't. I guess at times like that a person either gives up and goes under or tries real hard to swim to the surface. My precious Tara, still stuttering, gave me all of her love, but deep in my guts I knew that it was to be *me* and *me* alone who had to make the journey or not. I also knew that the last thing people remember you by is the last thing you do right before you die. And I really *didn't* want to be remembered by this or by future generations as a feeble, weak, out-of-control drunk. I just *didn't!*

It was by then, as six months go, right smack in the heart of our Lomar summer. And it was hot, very, very hot. I had cut my drinking a bit, but for sure I hadn't completely stopped. I was still out of work, and I was still getting those awful panic attacks. And I still wasn't driving. What happened to me *next* was on a Sunday, the seventh day of the week. Perhaps just an ordinary Sunday to some, but to me a turning point. I remember it so well, and I probably always will.

I was pushing Tara in our backyard swing. We had a *modest* backyard and a *modest* swing. I had put it together myself, and Tara really seemed to enjoy it. She had been through so much that no child should ever have to go through, and her swing was a place of forgetting for her. In my sober time, I would swing her, and we both really loved to do that. Like I said, the month was August, the day was Sunday. I hadn't shaved in days and I guess as shabby goes, I was brushed it. I was wearing a pair of sneakers without laces, and though it was so hot in August, I was still wearing this long, green, winter trench coat. Perhaps I wore it to cover some of my jagged scars, I don't know. Murphy's Law had tortured me, and my green trench coat maybe covered over some of my rips and claw marks. I had a bottle of very cheap wine in my left trench coat pocket. It was right then, right at the swing in my backyard, that I first heard *it*. *That voice*! There was *no* orange glow, and I *wasn't* drunk, and it *wasn't* a panic attack either. It was as real, as real could be. It *wasn't* a he voice and it *wasn't* a she voice. And it *wasn't* my Moll's voice either. It was simply *a voice*.

Of course it took me by surprise, as Tara and I were the only people actually there, but by then, though I had lost my faith in God, I *still* believed that there were things out there that truly existed, that just couldn't be scientifically explained—like *that voice* that day, that Sunday in August, in my thirty-fourth year on our good planet Earth.

"Walt, go back to your old baseball field!" That's *all* it said, and it only said it once.

But for me, at that exact time, at that exact place, and probably at that exact second, that voice was *exactly* what I needed. My old high school, where I had first met my Moll, and where I had found Coach Ray and baseball, had been closed down for a few years. Some industrial building was to take its place. Not a soul was there. My old high school, Lomar, wasn't far from my home with the swing. In fact nothing was far from anything in Lomar, Kansas.

As I, almost robo-like, followed the command of *that voice* back to my old stomping grounds, I got this terrific rush. And it wasn't one of those panic attack rushes that I had been getting. I was disheveled and had sleepers in my eyes from lack of sleep. As I arrived there and stared at the gray prison-like chain-link fence that now surrounded my old high school, I got this huge lump in my throat, and my eyes, with the sleepers, got misty. Standing there, I suddenly remembered *it all*. The dances, the pep rallies, my teachers, my first baseball glove, my folks, Coach Ray, and of course, my Molly. Tears were streaming down my unshaven face—oh how I remembered it all.

I followed the gray prison-like chain-link fence all the way around to the very back of the school. And there *it* was—and there *I* was, once again. I was standing right dab in front of my old baseball field. I was thirty-four or so on that day, and high school seemed almost all of the oceans away. The grass was discolored, the bases long gone, and the bleachers a lot decayed. But for sure, *the essence* of it all was still there. It didn't really matter *where* I sat in the bleachers, they were all completely empty, so I sat somewhere in the middle. I did take a few sips of the small bottle of wine I had in my green trench coat pocket, and I did start to read the newspaper that I had also brought from home with me. It was hot, real hot. And it, like I've said before, was Sunday, August 11, 1976. Being born on a certain September day back in 1942, that would have made me thirty-four years old, just what I've told you before. And being fifty-four *now*, I guess thirty-four was almost infancy—but infancy with a lot of six-month jagged scars.

I sat there in the bleachers, sipping, reading, and remembering, about the past and about the present. I *wasn't* thinking about any prospect of a future. What had happened to me and to my family in the last hundred and eighty days of my life was the worst of nightmares. One thing after the other, and among it all, the deaths of my son and of my wife. I had fallen into this huge black hole, and it seemed that there was no climbing up or ever getting out. And the two walls of the black hole were both starting to crush me. But sitting there that August day in my old baseball bleachers, I remembered so much. Coach Ray was so much more than just a baseball coach to me. I remembered him, and I remembered my old baseball number, eleven. I looked out to where centerfield use to be, and I laughingly remembered my very first catch from that Southgate guy, Meekin.

I remembered *a lot* sitting there that August Sunday, some twenty years ago now. I may not have been a very pretty sight, but for the first time in so very long, I was a little bit at peace. I'm not exactly sure *how* long I sat in the bleachers or *how* hot that August sun really was. We hadn't had a real Kansas dust storm in a long long time. And as far as I could tell none of the tell-tale forewarning signs were there.

Then out of nowhere, slowly but almost methodically the dust began to gather. But it didn't bother me, and even as it began to swirl thicker around me, I considered it, for some unholy reason, as almost my friend. For sure I remembered back to that horrible twister when I was only a kid, but for some reason on *that* day in *those* bleachers, I had no fear. Suddenly, in a wisp, the dust was *everywhere*. In my eyes, in my hair, in my nostrils, and even in my lace-less sneakers. It completely blanketed my green trench coat. Even my tiny bottle of wine and my newspaper were covered by it. I don't remember how long it lasted or how long it was supposed to last.

Thinking back now, I must have looked like a whole chimney exploded on top of me. I was a human dust ball. I also don't really remember exactly at what precise second the dust storm ended. It could have been seconds or even minutes. I'm sure it was less than a century. And I didn't care either. I wasn't having a panic attack. My Tara was safe back at her yard swing, and I just knew that from *that voice* on everything, and I mean everything, was to have a special reason. Anyway, when the dust did end, that second or that less than a century it was the very first time that I noticed *it—the date* on the top of my newspaper. It read August 11, 1876. I was *back* in time exactly one hundred years to the minute to the very second. There was *no* chain link fence, *no* baseball field, and *no* high school. The old bleachers were still there, and *I* was still there—that was it! And wilderness—there was lots and lots of wilderness. And a creek running through the wilderness. An actual, silver-like, unpolluted, gurgling creek. It looked exactly *how* it should have looked back in the year 1876.

I remember I was amazed and awed by everything. I was expectant, too. Like, *what* was to come next? That's when I heard *it, that voice* again. That voice that sent me back to my old baseball field to begin with. "Walt, dear, you're doing just fine. Now, follow the path!" And like in a trance, but not a trance, I did just that. I followed the path. It was as if the whole wilderness just upped and parted and right there in front of me, beckoning me, was this long dirt and gravel, August 11, 1876, path. I'm sure at the time I *didn't* feel like Moses at the Red Sea, I just felt like me. I stepped down from the bleachers and walked to the path—and I walked and I walked and I walked. I don't know for how far or for how long, I just kept on going.

And then I saw *it*. The *it*, was a *house*. And it was just as I would have imagined an 1876 wilderness house *should* have looked like. I was about twenty yards or so from it, and it appeared out of nowhere. But by then, I wasn't to be surprised or shocked by really anything. Like the date on the newspaper or the *path* or now even the *house*. The house had a chimney, and from where I stood, it all looked so warm and so inviting. It was August back then, too, *that* didn't change. The house also had a well in the front yard. I remember back then thinking, how nice that well water would have tasted on my dry lips. Maybe the owner of the house got their well water from the unpolluted gurgling brook that I had first seen or maybe not. Who did this house belong to? Did it belong to an 1876 *he* or an 1876 *she?* So many questions—would I ever get any answers?

As I was pondering the house and all of those possible questions, a man appeared in the front yard near the well—*an 1876 man.* It was quite obvious to me, though I was quite visible, that *he couldn't* see me, or perhaps *he wasn't* supposed to see me. He was a strong-looking, tanned, 1876 man. He seemed in his early forties. He was wearing work overalls and had a blue cap on his head. He had a fine handlebar moustache. He had huge arms with huger muscles. He was puffing on a corn cob pipe.

As I continued to watch, he started to put a horseshoe on his probably faithful horse—horses, *not* cars. I really *was* back in the 1800s! I was to find out but just a short time later that the man's name was *William Smith*—important or unimportant, his name had the *exact* same *initials* as mine: Walt Stillman, W.S. Mr. Smith was a part-time farmer and a part time bricklayer. He had lost both of his sons in the senseless civil war and had lost his wife, his loving soulmate, to the *back then* dreaded, tuberculosis. He, *too*, had a drinking problem. And also, exactly like me, he had a young daughter who had become *his* Rock of Gibraltar. Her name was Emily, not Tara.

Standing there that August day, I didn't really know that how or the what of how I knew all of that personal stuff about that man, but I just did. It was as if all of the important stuff about him was quickly *poured* into me. I'm, quite sure, looking back now, that I was totally invisible to them, as they showed absolutely *no* indication of my presence, none at all. It definitely appeared that Mr. Smith *also* suffered greatly at the hands of Murphy's Law, and also, like me, in a very short period of time. He had lost almost all of his beloved family to the war and to disease. His business was slowly fading, and drinking had surely become a part of his daily life. So much like what had happened to me, it was almost scary.

As Emily and her dad walked back to their cabin, *they* did it hand in hand. *I* followed a few yards behind. Was I finally going to find out about that voice that I had heard twice? Was I finally going to get some answers to my many many questions? My heart was racing with all kinds of anticipation.

I found myself in Mr. Smith's very own bedroom. It was as if I was just guided there. Of course it was a simple and plain bedroom, just like Mr. William Smith himself. And suddenly, there IT was, sitting on his wooden desk. It was a big brown *journal* with a huge golden clasp, a quill pen and an ink well right beside it. I slowly opened the clasp, and the very first page read: THIS IS THE LIFE OF ME, WILLIAM SMITH. Somehow I just didn't feel wrong at all about me being there or about doing that, not wrong at all.

I sat down in his very desk chair and I read and I read and I read. I read all of Mr. Smith's journal. He wrote about almost *everything*— his early life, his parents, his wife, his children, the Civil War—he wrote about it *all*. When I read what he wrote, about the loss of his boys and of his wife, I could feel his anger, and it was *toward God*. He was very, very hurt and very, very angry. As I read on, I couldn't stop. I almost *had* to keep on reading. His journal pages *weren't* numbered, so I don't know exactly what page *it* was on, but *it* surely was there, scribbled with his very own quill pen—"Hey, God, are you really, really up there?" *He* WROTE one hundred years *before* exactly what *I* had, in the last six months, twice SAID!

I was frozen in his wooden desk chair. What the heck was going on? What the heck was happening? As I recovered and slowly read on, I began to notice a tremendous *change*. Mr. Smith was thawing out— his ice towards God was melting. In his journal, in his very own words, page after page, the *skeptic* was becoming the *believer*. Maybe *that's why* I was sent there. This pioneer man, who had so much hurt just like me, was slowly changing. Some of his words and thoughts *weren't* in order, but somehow I understood them. He wrote that good is good, and that bad *also* can be good. *That* was a mouthful for me to swallow, that bad can *ever* be good! But again, it made total sense to me. It was bad that England had hurt us, back in the colonial days, but in a way it was also good, because it made us declare our freedom. He wrote that bad makes us strive to do better, and that bad makes us *appreciate* the good when it jumps right up and smacks us in the head! In Vietnam, I went for long periods of time without food or drink or even a shower, but *now*, even years and years later, a hot shower with lots and lots of water is really and fully appreciated by me. He wrote that we never take the time to thank God in the good times, but always complain to God at the first sight of trouble. He wrote that *God doesn't* cause any bad, he simply created us and we ourselves cause the bad. He created us to figure out what to do if and when the bad begins to happen.

By the time I had finished Mr. Smith's journal *I*, like *him*, had almost thawed out. And for sure it was a good thaw. Did I really go back in time one hundred years? Was there really a Mr. William Smith and his young daughter Emily? I remember thinking about every time as a kid when I had read the *Christmas Story* by Charles Dickens. Was there really a ghost of Christmas future or did old Ebenezer create him all by his very own self? Did *I* create my very own *William Smith*? Or did William Smith go back in time himself and meet someone else to give *him* his answers, too? But none of that really matters. What does matter is from that very moment on, I was going to live each and every day of my life, as Mr. Smith had almost told me to—*with faith*! *That*, to me, was to be eternally for certain.

Epilogue

And again, out of nowhere, I was back—back in the bleachers of my old Lomar High baseball field. It was all just exactly as if I had *never* left. There was *no* dust, *no* wilderness, *no* gurgling creek, and certainly *no* Mr. William Smith and his young daughter Emily. And the date on the newspaper was once again August 11, 1976. I was *still* thirty-four years old.

Everything said and done, all the ifs or whys forgotten, I am *NOW* fifty-four. Twenty years or so have passed since it all happened, which would make it just about 1996—although, as you well know, I'm not much good on things like dates. I certainly have more wrinkles now, my teeth *aren't* all mine, and I do smoke a corncob pipe. I surely *don't* drink anymore and I *don't* go out on dates, either, though I do have some friends who happen to be women. My Moll was *thee* magnificent act and to even try to follow or to try to imitate that, would have been an injustice to all concerned. I also *haven't* had one of those old panic attacks in going on twenty years.

My folks, Walter Sr. and Melinda, though a bit older, are wonderfully alive and still occupy their Stillman Farm. On occasion I still go to *our* old tree, and on a fairly regular basis I plant some lilacs at the grave of my Moll and my Chadster. Some things just never did change, nor do I ever want them to. I never did go back to work at the electric company motor pool. The people there were more than great to me during and after all of my troubles. I will never, ever forget their love and their warmth. But I chose to work at making and building

82

things, like a beautiful hobby horse, for the kids of Lomai who were a little less fortunate than most in one way or another, just like my Mall used to do yours before. I am as happy as a fifty-five year old man could be who smokes his corncob, never forgets where or who he came from, and totally has his faith back.

My Tara, like me, is *also* older by the same twenty years. She no longer stutters. She has a wonderful job and an adoring husband—not to my surprise, she married another fellow Kansian. Together they have made me the proudest of grandpops. My grandson's almost name, or at least what everybody calls him, is "MiC." *I* even call him that. Tara named him for her mother, Molly, and her brother, Chad. And every time MiC teaches me something new about life, or I simply get the loving chance to smell him or to smother him with grandpop kisses, there is *one thing* that is absolutely, assuredly, and abundantly for certain—that whether or not God is a he God or a she God, whether or not God is a young God or an old God, that *one thing* that to me, finally is for eternally certain: God is indeed really, really up there!

El Fin - or not?